THE CABAL

POWELL BOOK 6

Bill Ward

"Nearly all men can stand adversity, but if you want to
test a man's character, give him power."

Abraham Lincoln

CHAPTER ONE

The wealthy American businessman was flying to Singapore for an important meeting. He was pleased to be getting out of the country. Although it was a business trip, he would have time to enjoy some female company and generally relax. He was staying in a suite at one of his favourite hotels in all the world. He was a regular guest at the famous Raffles hotel and was well known to all the staff.

He planned to spend two days in meetings with bankers and then a further two days partying. It was self-indulgent and extremely extravagant. The cost was not an issue but he rarely took time away from work. He had told his staff only to contact him in an emergency. Should anyone wrongly judge what constituted an emergency, they would be looking for a new job.

He wasn't travelling with his usual entourage. He was having high level meetings, which didn't require the presence of his lieutenants. If the meetings went well, then they would get involved. He had just the one bodyguard with him, who was the soul of discretion. Which was fortunate, as the gutter press would pay a tidy sum for what he knew. Of course, he was well paid but others had succumbed to temptation and been lured to sell their stories of debauchery. You couldn't put a price on loyalty.

The hotel had organised a driver to pick them up from the airport and be available for the duration of his stay. As they exited the arrivals hall, the driver could be clearly seen holding up the name Briggs, which was the bodyguard's name. The businessman didn't need to advertise his arrival.

They were led outside by the driver and walked into a wall of heat. It was a familiar but unwelcome feeling as business regularly took him to the Middle East and Asia. He wasn't the tallest man and too many expensive dinners had left their mark around his midriff. The heat made him sweat profusely. It was an undignified scenario, he didn't enjoy.

The driver led the way to a very large Mercedes. The driver scurried around holding open doors and making sure the bags were properly stacked in the boot. He had a friendly smile permanently affixed to his face.

The driver kept respectfully silent during the thirty minute drive to the hotel. The air conditioning gave respite from the furnace like heat on the streets. The businessman made a couple of calls back home to Texas. The first call was to speak with his wife and confirm he had arrived safely. A longer call to his office established there was no change to his itinerary and nothing else urgent needing his attention.

The last few weeks had been extra stressful and he needed the break. He had come close to accepting an invitation to join an elite group of people, who were trying to change the world. He'd given it a great deal of thought and decided in the end it was too idealistic a notion. The world couldn't be changed by a handful of people, no matter how rich.

Generally, he believed any problem could be solved if you hit it over the head with a large enough sack of money but this was different. There were too many national and religious obstacles. Anyway, he was getting a bit too old to try and change the world. Perhaps if he had children, he would think differently.

His friend, who had offered the invitation, had not taken the rejection well. He had tried to hide his disappointment but had obviously taken it as a personal insult and they had ended up arguing. What concerned the businessman was that his friend was very close to the new President. He detested the President but he wasn't someone you wanted as your enemy.

When they arrived at the hotel, he remained seated on the backseat to give the driver time to jump out and open his door. Then he stepped out of the car just behind his bodyguard. He was hit again by the extreme heat and happy once they were inside the air conditioned hotel.

He hung back as his bodyguard approached the desk to announce his arrival and complete the formalities. The hotel foyer wasn't terribly busy. One man approached the desk from behind the businessman. He stumbled and reached out his hand, using the businessman's shoulder to steady himself.

"I'm terribly sorry," the man apologised in an Irish accent. "The floor is slippery."

"No problem."

The Irishman walked up to the front desk and picked up a map of the city from a pile of tourist information on one side of the desk. When he turned around, the businessman was perspiring even more than usual and becoming very red in the face. He was clutching his heart with his hand.

The Irishman was happy with what he saw. The businessman would be dead within minutes. The needle containing the toxin had been hidden in the palm of the Irishman's hand. He had delivered it to the back of the businessman's neck when he pretended to lose balance. The empty, small syringe was now safely stored inside his jacket pocket.

The Irishman walked past the businessman without a second glance. As he reached the hotel exit, he removed the thin latex gloves, which he had been wearing. He could hear over his shoulder, the beginnings of a commotion back in the foyer. He hailed a taxi and asked to be taken to the airport.

CHAPTER TWO

Powell was having lunch with Angela Bennett, in a very smart restaurant in the heart of Covent Garden, famous for serving some of the best sea food in London. The place was full and noisy with the chatter of diners, who in their smart suits, looked for the most part like they were business people, escaping the office to discuss important deals.

It had been a couple of years since Powell helped rescue Angela's two children from Saudi Arabia, where they had been abducted by her husband. She had exhausted legitimate legal processes and as a last resort turned to Powell for help. It had been a difficult operation for Powell but he eventually achieved a successful outcome. Angela's ex-husband was now dead and she no longer lived in fear of reprisals.

Everything about Angela was always the epitome of a privileged upbringing. She was an extremely wealthy woman. She was wearing an expensive purple dress, which Powell assumed was from a well-known designer. She would do her shopping in Bond Street not on the high street. There was never a hair out of place and she wore a beautiful pearl necklace, which was probably purchased at Cartier or somewhere similar. She spoke with an upper class accent and was the product of expensive private schools. Powell's upbringing had been far less privileged but he genuinely liked Angela. Despite her wealth, she was very down to earth. Powell always enjoyed their lunches.

As Powell studied the menu, he tried to mask his astonishment at the prices. The restaurant was charging three times as much as he charged for the same fish, in his bar in Brighton. He was pretty sure it came from the same sea and doubted it would taste three times as good. Not that the prices were a cause for any concern. He wouldn't be paying the bill. He had given up a long time ago trying to get

Angela to let him pay for lunch. It no longer made him feel uncomfortable. It wasn't just that she was rich. She had said many times, she would forever be indebted to him for returning her children. Paying for lunch was just a small way of saying thank you.

After ordering their food, Powell glanced across the table and could sense Angela had something on her mind. They normally met every three months for a lunch, to keep in touch. As it had only been six weeks since their last lunch, he had been surprised to receive the latest invitation. He had wondered if there was a specific reason Angela wanted to meet. At previous lunches she had been very light hearted but today the sparkle was definitely missing.

"Is there a problem?" Powell probed. "You don't seem yourself."

Angela gave a little cough to clear her throat. "I'm trying to decide whether to burden you with yet another problem. It seems unfair to keep asking for your help."

"Are the children okay?" Powell asked concerned.

"They are fine. This relates to a female friend of mine."

"What's her name?"

"I'm not sure I should tell you. First let me explain the problem. Then you can decide whether you want to know her name."

Powell was intrigued. "As you wish."

At that moment the waiter appeared with the white wine they had ordered. Powell could feel the suspense building as they sat in silence, while the waiter correctly described the Chablis they had ordered and showed Powell the bottle to confirm it was indeed the right one.

Then the waiter went through the process of removing the foil and the cork. He poured a little of the wine for Powell to taste, which he did quickly and confirmed it was satisfactory. He didn't bother pointing out Angela had chosen the wine and should really be doing the taste test. The waiter then half filled their glasses before returning the bottle to a bucket of ice. The whole episode seemed to take for ever.

As soon as the waiter departed, Angela immediately raised her glass to her lips without a toast and almost drained the glass. Powell raised an eyebrow. Angela was acting completely out of character. He refilled her glass.

"My friend is married to a politician," Angela explained. "Quite a well-known one actually. She recently told me in confidence about something she stumbled across. I promised her I wouldn't breathe a word to anyone but I need to tell someone."

"Does it involve her husband?"

"Yes and that's the problem. She loves her husband but what she's discovered suggests he is mixed up in something terrible."

"Has she spoken to her husband?"

"No. She's afraid how he will react. It seems he has quite a temper at the best of times. And they have two lovely children."

"So what did she discover?" Powell prompted. His mind flashed back to Bob Hale, the MP he was protecting who turned out to be a paedophile. There had been a suggestion other politicians might be involved.

"I don't want to put you in more danger. I would never be able to forgive myself if…" She left the sentence unfinished and helped herself to some more wine.

"You know I can take care of myself," Powell replied reassuringly. He was genuinely intrigued to hear what had caused Angela to become so concerned for his welfare. "Tell me everything you know and then we can discuss what to do next. What's the saying? A problem shared is a problem halved."

Angela looked him straight in the eyes. "I guess I wouldn't have arranged this lunch if I didn't intend to ask for your help." She leaned forward, resting her forearms on the table. "For some time my friend has suspected her husband of having an affair. She's caught him out lying about where he's been and who he has been with. It's mostly a series of small clues. She's an intelligent woman and I trust her judgement."

Powell had thought he was going to be hearing more than a story about a philandering politician. It wasn't his area of expertise. "I'm not really sure I want to get mixed up in someone's marriage problems."

"This isn't about their marriage. She wanted to find proof of his infidelity so she started snooping into his personal affairs." Angela hesitated for a moment, knowing she had reached the point of no return. "Are you sure you want me to go on? You mustn't feel obligated to help."

"Angela, just tell me what you know," Powell implored. "Then I can make a decision."

She took a deep breath and tried to edge even closer across the table. She checked to either side to make sure no one could overhear what she was about to say. "My friend's name is Rose. I've known her for ten years. We met when her husband was first elected to Parliament. They moved to London and she was desperately lonely. I don't know what she ever saw in that dreadful man. He's an arrogant bully." The wine was encouraging Angela to be more forthright in her views.

"And who exactly is her husband?"

"George Carter."

"I know who he is," Powell confirmed. He recognised the name, despite only a limited interest in politics. Carter was known for his very right wing views and was one of the few willing to voice support for the new and deeply unpopular American President.

"Everyone does," Angela sighed. "Anyway, Rose is quite computer savvy and searched her husband's computer. It seems he uses the same password for almost everything. She found he has a secret email account. She says, she saw an email sent to him, which had a speech attached that whoever wrote the email, said he should give after the attack on the church in Hammersmith."

The recent attack on the church by a lone Muslim gunman had resulted in the deaths of three people and several more injured. It would have been worse if two armed police officers hadn't been responding to a call very nearby. They had shot and killed the terrorist.

As a result of the attack, there had been a softening of criticism of the American President's strict new anti-Muslim travel bans. People were outraged that the gunman had arrived in the country as a refugee from Syria. George Carter had suggested the Prime Minister should follow the lead of the American President and put stricter controls on refugees entering the country.

"That's not unusual," Powell replied. "Most politicians have speech writers."

"You don't understand. The email was sent the day before the attack."

CHAPTER THREE

The Chairman called the meeting to order. A buffet lunch had been prepared and the five businessmen, some of whom had travelled a very long way, helped themselves to a plate of food before taking their seats at the large, round table. The Chairman was a great fan of Arthurian legend and the shape of the table was a conscious choice. He saw himself as a King Arthur figure. He had assembled his knights, who were well equipped to slay modern day dragons.

The men sat around the table owned a quarter of the world's wealth. Together that amounted to approximately two hundred and fifty billion dollars. On average, each man owned as much as four hundred million people. While the men around the table kept getting richer, the poor and even the middle classes were being left behind.

Outsiders would undoubtedly look upon them with suspicion so secrecy was essential. If the press became aware of their existence, the scrutiny and publicity would make it impossible to operate effectively. That would be undeserved as the Cabal had not been established out of self-interest. As six of the wealthiest men on the planet, obtaining further wealth was not their driving aim. They had loftier ambitions.

The men at the table were not generally business competitors. The Chairman had not wanted there to be any conflict of interest between their business interests and the needs of the group. The Chairman was a banker. Others represented everything from energy to publishing and technology brands. They were all global businesses that wielded huge influence. Their businesses, in one way or another, touched upon the lives of virtually every person on the planet.

The Chairman had always been ambitious and in his youth had dreamed of building a global business empire. He was the son of a banker and enjoyed a privileged upbringing but he was not satisfied with being a big fish in a small pond. He wanted to be a big fish in the ocean. He had grown the bank to become one of the largest investment banks in the world, which led to the accumulation of enormous personal wealth.

With the passing of time and the growing recognition of his mortality, making more money was no longer able to satisfy his ambition. He had decided to put all his energies into helping mankind, which seemed embarked on a path to self-destruction.

As a start, it was necessary to eradicate terrorism, which was dragging the world back into the dark ages. The Chairman had recognised this could not be achieved within the constrictions of the current political establishment. Democracy had allowed terrorism to flourish and without intervention, the men around the table believed a catastrophe was inevitable.

It was time for action not more words. Action on a global scale, not limited by country borders and the petty agendas of politicians, who would always be focused first on their national problems and re-election. It was a massive undertaking and would be a fitting legacy to leave behind as the Chairman reached the latter stages of his life.

The Chairman had thought long and hard about who he should invite to have a seat at the table. A couple of old friends had been easy choices but the other invitations had been based on a thorough examination of each man's values and integrity. The Chairman was not looking for individuals attracted by the idea of further wealth or power. All of the men at the table already gave generously to charity. That in itself was expected given their wealth. More importantly, they ran ethical businesses and were concerned about their imprint on the planet.

This was to be a crusade to improve the world and the Chairman was under no illusions about the task that lay ahead or the time it would take to achieve. He did not expect to see everything achieved in what remained of his lifetime. They were about sowing seeds and he expected it would be the next generation who saw his dreams flower.

He considered he had chosen his team well and only one man had rebuffed his approach, despite initially seeming to be interested. Despite their friendship, he had learned too much of the Chairman's plans and shortly after announcing he was no longer interested in their undertaking, he had taken a business trip to Singapore and never returned. He was pronounced dead from a heart attack. His death was not considered suspicious and the men sat at the table weren't even aware of the fate they would suffer, were they to ever have a sudden change of heart.

The Chairman's conscience was barely pricked by the man's death, which was an unfortunate consequence of the need to maintain absolute secrecy. Others may also have to be sacrificed before the Cabal's aims were realised but no one ever made an omelette without breaking some eggs.

If the men around the table were his knights, there were many others recruited into the organisation to provide specific services. They were mostly practical choices where values were less important than what they could deliver. The men at the table were solely responsible for strategy. It was the job of the others to execute components of the plan.

Once everyone was seated, the Chairman spoke first. "This is a very exciting time in our history. We have never been better placed to achieve our goals. It is time for the next stage of our plan. Carter's speech was very well received. He is making rapid progress towards becoming leader. And the recent attacks on London simply help further his position. The current Prime Minister's incompetence is working out better for us than any action we could plan. However, I do have one concern…"

The remaining men immediately focused on the Chairman and ignored their food. If the Chairman had a concern, then for certain they too had reason to be concerned.

The Chairman continued, now he had everyone's full attention. "The press continues to give our friend in the White House a torrid time. It seems like the whole world is against him."

"He doesn't exactly help himself," the Englishman present commented. He was approaching seventy years of age and never short of an opinion. "If he insists on waging war on the press, they aren't going to take it lying down."

There was a murmur of agreement from the others at the table.

"I'm not sure we should have encouraged him to withdraw from the Paris climate accord," the Chinese industrialist stated. "I know I was a strong advocate for doing so but the President's actions are turning the whole world against him. He is no use to us if he is kicked out after one term."

"That's if he survives a full term," the Englishman added. He had never liked the American and couldn't understand how he managed to be elected. He was far too brash and lacked any political experience.

"It is his combatant style that helped get him elected," the Chairman interjected smoothly. "We all supported him knowing full well what to expect." The Chairman looked at each individual, challenging anyone to disagree. The President had been a member of the inner circle from the early days. He had proposed that he should run for President and his success had come as something of a surprise.

"What you say is correct," the Russian in the room agreed. He was the youngest man in the room, being a self-made billionaire rather than having been born into money. "But these investigations into his relationship with Putin go far beyond what was anticipated. Putin is worried if the truth comes out that the West will impose further sanctions. We cannot afford to lose Putin's goodwill."

"Unfortunately that is something outside of our immediate control," the Chairman answered. "We have to tread carefully. We will call in favours with our friends in the Senate if it proves necessary but for the time being, we have to let the investigations run their course."

The Russian didn't look satisfied but said nothing further.

The Chairman continued, "There is one thing certain to make the country rally round and support the President..."

The men around the table looked at each other uncertainly.

"Reduce taxes?" the Russian suggested.

"No. That's not economically viable. I have come up with a more personal solution to the problem. An assassination attempt." The Chairman made it sound like an everyday event.

Glances were exchanged around the table. Had they heard correctly?

"You mean, we are going to have someone shoot your President?" the Chinese man said incredulously. "Has he agreed to this?"

"I haven't discussed it with him yet."

"I'm not sure you should," the Englishman said. "I can't imagine he will be too happy about the idea." Secretly, the Englishman thought it was a brilliant idea.

"We are only talking a very slight wound. He will be a national hero. I think that will appeal to him."

"Perhaps we shouldn't tell him," the Russian said.

"That wouldn't be right," the Chairman replied. In truth, he had thought of not telling the President but that would make the whole operation far riskier. He needed to be on board with the plan. Otherwise, he risked moving at the wrong moment and ending up with a bullet in his heart instead of his shoulder.

"What if he doesn't agree?" the German asked. "Do you have a backup plan?"

"I've known the President a long time. I am quite certain he will see the merit in my plan."

"It's an audacious and quite brilliant idea," the Chinese man said. "Please note for future reference that in my country this would not work. There would simply be a terrible purge." Then he added, "However, I am sure it would work very well in Germany and Russia." He smiled and looked at the German and Russian sat at the table.

"I don't think the idea has the same merit if you are just a businessman," the German replied, quite seriously.

"He is only joking," the Russian said.

The Chairman was pleased to see his idea had no opposition. Then again, none of the men at the table were going to be shot. He continued, "After all the recent terrorist attacks in the UK, they are crying out for new leadership and Carter is looking well placed to step up to the plate. If we can cement the President's position then we really are in very good shape."

"When and where is this going to take place?" the Englishman asked.

"I'm still working on the details," the Chairman replied. "I just wanted you all to know what I was thinking and ask you to allow me to proceed with the detailed planning without further discussion. Security will evidently be critical."

"There will be a huge short term drop in the markets when he is shot. It would be useful to have some idea of the date so we can prepare," the Englishman said. "We could even make a killing."

"It is vital none of us does anything to reveal we expected an assassination attempt," the Chairman cautioned. "We do not try to make short term gains out of this plan. Sit tight and the markets will recover soon enough."

CHAPTER FOUR

Powell's first inclination was to believe Rose Carter had simply made a mistake. She had confused the dates. Or perhaps there was a technical glitch and the email had the wrong date? There had to be a simple explanation.

"So Rose has only told you about this?" Powell queried. "She hasn't said a word to her husband or anyone else?"

"She's only told me," Angela confirmed. "And she doesn't know I've told you."

"What was she expecting you to do about it?"

"Nothing. It was just driving her mad not being able to tell anyone. She doesn't have many friends. Her husband never lets her out of the house."

"Perhaps she made a mistake. You haven't actually seen the email?"

"No. But I believe the email exists. She isn't lying."

"When did she tell you about this?"

"Two days ago. I slept on it and then called you yesterday morning to arrange this lunch."

"If I'm to help, I need to take a look at the email."

"Why don't we drop by her place after lunch for coffee? Saves you making a second visit up to town."

"Okay. Give her a call and see if she's in."

"Actually, I already did and she's expecting me."

Powell smiled. "That's very…" He searched for the right word. "Organised of you."

"The word you really wanted was devious," Angela laughed.

"I could never think of you as devious. You were just being practical. Will she mind me tagging along?"

"No. She knows all about you. I've told her about how you saved my children. She always said she would love to meet you."

"I assume there's no chance of her husband being at home?"

"No. I checked and he won't be back until late."

They enjoyed the remainder of their lunch and Powell kept the conversation away from the subject of Rose Carter. It was evident Angela had a great affection for Rose and hated her husband. More than once she hinted that Rose was subjected to physical abuse. Powell didn't want her views clouding his judgement. He would meet Rose and form his own opinions.

They skipped desert as Angela explained her friend always served cake with coffee. After a ten minute taxi journey, they were being shown into Rose's sitting room, in a mews house in Knightsbridge. Powell had never really understood the desire of the rich to pay ridiculous amounts of money for a property in a narrow street with little parking and small rooms. Perhaps they all fled to country mansions for the weekend.

"I've heard so much about you?" Rose said, offering a cup of coffee to Powell. There was only a hint of a Yorkshire accent.

She looked like a younger version of Angela. There was the same slim figure, elegance, expensive clothes and jewellery. Her short blonde hair framed a pretty face but the makeup didn't quite hide the dark bags under her eyes. He knew from Angela, Rose was in her early forties but to his eye, she looked a few years younger.

He'd seen her husband on the television and wondered what was the attraction. George Carter certainly wasn't what anyone would call handsome. Had she been attracted by his money and position? He realised he was jumping to conclusions with no basis in fact but it did seem a mismatch. Perhaps it was true love? Who was he to pass judgement on other people's love lives?

"I hope you don't mind me coming," Powell apologised. "I was having lunch with Angela and she said you wouldn't mind."

"Of course I don't mind. In fact, I've been looking forward to meeting you. It isn't often you get to meet a real life super hero."

Powell almost blushed at the description. "I think you have me confused with someone else."

"Not according to Angela."

"She exaggerates," Powell answered, glancing at Angela and admonishing her by nodding his head from side to side.

"You've told him. Haven't you?" Rose queried, sitting back in her chair and looking at Angela.

Angela looked uncertain for a moment before deciding to be honest. "Powell can help," she replied positively. "He'll know what to do."

"If you think I'm interfering, I can just finish my coffee and never speak of this again," Powell offered.

"To be honest, I'm glad you are here," Rose encouraged. "I've been going mad wondering what to do. I can't sleep and can't concentrate on anything."

"Have you spoken to your husband?" Powell asked.

"And tell him what? I was sneaking through his computer because I thought he was having an affair and then I discovered he might be mixed up in terrorism. He's a difficult man at the best of times. Anyway, he would just deny everything."

"Can you show me the email?"

"What are you going to do after I show you it?"

"What do you want me to do?"

"I know what I don't want you to do. I don't want my husband to learn I was responsible for discovering the email."

"I'll do my best. He may be suspicious but if you keep calm and deny any knowledge, then he may believe he's been hacked. In fact, I can speak to someone I know, who might be able to help support that theory."

"Will you promise to do nothing without first consulting with me?"

"I have to be honest. If you show me the email and I believe it indicates your husband is mixed up in terrorism, then I can't just pretend it doesn't exist."

"So once I show you the email, I've really let the cat out of the bag. There's no going back?"

Powell didn't reply. It was a statement of the reality not a question.

"Show Powell the email," Angela encouraged. "He will know what to do."

"Seems I have little choice," Rose sighed. "Rather like Powell, I can't forget what I've seen. Come with me to the office."

Rose sat at the desk and the others stood behind her, one on each side looking over her shoulders. It became apparent after a couple of minutes that Rose was having trouble finding the email.

"It's gone," Rose admitted after a further minute of frantic searching. "Perhaps the bloody thing was just a figment of my imagination."

Powell could see they were in an email system he'd never heard of called Protonmail and George Carter had the user name SaintGeorge.

"Do you mind if I take a look?" Powell asked.

Rose stood up and indicated for Powell to take her chair.

There were several old emails, which Powell read but they were only confirmation of meetings in different locations. They were all sent from the same email account – thechairman@Protonmail.com. Powell then searched the sent and deleted boxes but there was nothing of interest.

"Could your husband have any reason to suspect you've been looking at his computer?" Powell asked, turning to Rose.

"No. Definitely not."

"Then perhaps he just did the sensible thing and deleted the email."

Powell had a sudden thought. He looked on the desktop to find the Recycle Bin. He double clicked and up came a Word document called Speech.doc.

"That's it," Rose exclaimed. "I thought I was going mad."

"We may have hit the jackpot," Powell said excitedly.

He hovered over the document and found himself staring at the date it was created. It was the day before the terrorist attack. He restored the document and then opened it to confirm it was the speech to be given after the terrorist attack. Powell took out his phone and took a picture of the screen.

"So now you both believe me?" Rose asked with a sense of relief.

"I never doubted you," Angela answered.

Powell deleted the document again, leaving it in the Recycle Bin. Then he closed the email and turned off the computer.

"What are you going to do?" Rose asked.

"I'm not sure. Leave it with me while I do some digging around. Try to carry on with your normal life and don't say anything to anyone," Powell warned. "Especially not to your husband."

CHAPTER FIVE

Powell was uncertain what to do next. He decided he needed to speak with Brian, his old friend at MI5. Working in conjunction with the police, they would be closely involved in the investigation into the attack on the church. Although the shooter was dead, they would need to determine whether the terrorist was working alone or was part of a wider cell. If it was the latter, then further attacks were a possibility.

There were many questions needed answering. Where did the terrorist get his weapon? Did he have help with planning the attack? Powell had a new question to throw into the mix. Had MI5 discovered anything that could lend credence to the idea a Member of Parliament could somehow be involved? It seemed far-fetched to say the least.

After leaving Rose and Angela, Powell called Brian and stressed it was essential they meet before he returned to Brighton. Brian didn't waste time with superfluous questions and suggested a pub on Vauxhall Bridge Road, only five minutes from his office.

Brian was standing at the bar with a pint in hand when Powell arrived.

"You're starting early," Powell admonished Brian good naturedly, as they shook hands.

"So would you in my place," Brian replied. "Everyone is working minimum twelve hour days at the moment. What can I get you?"

"I'll have the same as you."

"I thought you said it was a bit early?"

"I've been out to lunch so this is more a continuation than a beginning."

Brian ordered Powell's pint and they went to sit at a table in the corner. It being late afternoon, the pub was almost empty.

"Thanks for meeting so quickly," Powell said.

"It sounded important," Brian replied. "And to be honest, I fancied a break from the office."

"How is the investigation into the church shootings going?" Powell asked, getting straight to the point.

Brian became extra attentive. "We haven't made much progress but it's still early days. We're retracing his steps from Syria. Why do you ask?"

Powell described his day so far but omitted Rose's name.

"Are we talking about George Carter?" Brian suddenly asked.

"What makes you say that?" Powell was shocked and intrigued by Brian's response.

"His speech received a great deal of coverage. It was very impressive and won him a load of new admirers. It was supposed to be off the cuff but now I'm wondering if it was actually written in advance."

"It was George Carter," Powell confirmed.

"Shit! Are you absolutely certain it isn't just a wrong date on a document?"

"Fairly positive. I can send you a copy of what I found on his computer." Powell took out his phone and sent Brian the photo he'd taken of the speech. "Whatever the date, it's still pretty weird. He was pretending to speak from his heart but he didn't even write the speech. It wouldn't go down very well with the public."

"So who sent Carter the speech?" Brian asked as he studied the photo.

"I don't have any real idea but someone calling himself the Chairman, sent the email. I saw various other emails organising regular meetings with this Chairman. From what I read, it seems other people also attended these meetings."

"How many other people?"

"I don't know but in one email, the Chairman asked everyone to be punctual as he had another important meeting to go to afterwards. I didn't see their email addresses so they must have been blind copied."

"Everyone sounds like more than just one or two."

"I'd say at least four and quite possibly more."

"Carter isn't the sort of guy to bow down to just anyone. If this Chairman is pulling Carter's strings, then it's safe to assume the Chairman is someone with a great deal of power and influence."

"That's what I was thinking and it's why I wanted to meet you so urgently. I don't suppose MI5 have heard any whispers about Carter or a secret group?"

"Not that I know of but then I wouldn't need to know. I'll see what I can find out."

"Tread carefully," Powell cautioned. "We don't know who can be trusted and don't mention anything about the speech. It could be putting Rose Carter's life in danger. Whoever these people are, they're playing for high stakes. If they had anything to do with the terrorist attack, they aren't going to leave any witnesses alive."

"I'll be careful. Make sure Rose Carter and Angela don't say a word to anyone else. We need to keep a very tight lid on this until we know exactly what we're dealing with."

"Agreed."

CHAPTER SIX

The Chairman looked out from the window of his office, high above Manhattan. From his towering vantage point, the people below looked like ants, scurrying about their business. He was the equivalent of the queen bee as thousands toiled daily to ensure his business flourished. The traffic looked gridlocked but the police would ensure his guest had a trouble free journey across town.

The Chairman turned from the window as the intercom on his desk buzzed. "Yes, Lauren."

"He has arrived and is on his way up," the personal assistant announced.

Despite his visitor's lofty position, the Chairman wasn't intimidated by the President. They had known each other for fifty years and their families had been doing business for close to a hundred years. The Chairman's support and contacts had been instrumental in helping get him elected.

When the President entered the office, he was accompanied by various staff. They had been greeted downstairs by the Chairman's Executive Vice President of Investment Banking, who had personally worked with the President on a large number of deals over many years.

"Good to see you, Mr. President," the Chairman greeted his visitor. He didn't like being deferential to anyone but in front of the others he needed to be formal.

They shook hands and both of them went through the ritual of gripping extra firmly as if trying to assert their superiority. After the brief pleasantries, the President asked everyone to clear the room as the meeting was to be a one on one with the Chairman. The Secret Service agents were ushered outside with the promise of coffee and pastries.

With the door closed on the rest of the world, the Chairman guided his visitor to the comfortable chairs in the corner of the huge office.

The President smiled. "I'm afraid I can't stay long, Ted. I'm meeting later with the Attorney General, to finalise plans for keeping our country safe from terrorists. I don't want any problems with the courts this time."

"I guess you're learning it's not easy being President."

"You're not kidding. In business I tell someone what I want doing and it gets done. The President of the United States is supposed to be the most powerful man on the planet but I can't get any legislation passed."

"At least the papers aren't being so negative to your ideas since the most recent attack in London."

"True. That has been a stroke of good luck."

"Not entirely down to luck."

"It took a second for the President to realise the significance of the Chairman's comment. "Do you mean?"

"Yes."

"Why didn't you let me know what you were planning?"

"Plausible deniability. I didn't want there to be any possible evidence of you being involved. You sound more credible when you're not having to lie."

"So why are you telling me now then?"

"Telling you what? I've told you nothing." The Chairman had wanted the President to know because it was a reminder of how indebted he was to the Chairman and the others. The President was a bit of a wild card and needed keeping on a short leash. "Let's get down to business. I've spoken with our friend in Moscow and he seeks final confirmation you won't interfere in the Baltic."

"Quid pro quo. He helped get me elected. I look after my friends. We won't interfere in the Baltic states, wherever the hell they are."

The Chairman wasn't entirely convinced the President was joking about the location of the Baltic states. "I'll relay your confirmation to

Moscow. It will be some months before this happens. It will start with some unrest and protests from the local Russians already living in the Baltic. A bit like what happened in the Ukraine."

"I shall tell the American people it's a problem for Europe, not us. It's about time they started pulling their weight. We need to focus on things closer to home. The Muslim extremists are our real enemy not the Russians. We need to get a grip on immigration."

"You don't need to convince me," the Chairman interrupted. Not for the first time, the President had started to sound like he was making a speech at one of his rallies. "By the way, it's good to see your ratings are improving."

"I never doubted they would. Before long, I bet I have the best ratings of any President ever. And I'm not going to let the press and their fake news say differently."

The Chairman didn't entirely share the President's confidence. Voters could be very fickle and the press were a huge influence on public opinion. "Actually, I'd like to discuss some ideas for improving your ratings. I think I've come up with an idea to send them soaring through the roof."

"Really?"

Yes. Really."

"Well I'd sure like to hear about that."

The Chairman smiled broadly. "It's a simple idea. We have someone shoot you."

CHAPTER SEVEN

Powell was in his bar, eating what he deemed to be a late breakfast but many would call an early lunch. He was trying not to stare too hard at the new waitress. She was truly stunning and he had to force himself to look away. As he did so his eyes met Afina, who was looking at him with a knowing smile as she approached his table.

"You obviously approve of my new recruit," Afina said.

"She seems very capable"

Afina laughed. "She's a good worker as well as being very pretty."

"I hadn't noticed."

"Really. Perhaps I'd better make an appointment for you to have your eyes tested."

"Very funny. Want to join me for a coffee?"

Afina took a seat. "Adie, can you get me a large latte please," she called out to the pretty new girl. She turned to Powell. "Do you want another one?"

"Please."

"Adie, make that two, please."

Adie smiled and headed towards the bar.

"Where is Adie from?" Powell asked.

"She is Romanian. From Bucharest."

"Why are you grinning?"

"She asked if you were a good boss and I lied. I told her you are very nice."

Powell smiled at the compliment. "I still don't see the joke."

Adie reappeared with the coffees. "Hello Powell," she said, putting the coffees down on the table.

"Hello Adie. Welcome to Brighton. Is it your first time in England?"

"Don't you recognise me?" Adie asked.

"It can't be!" Powell suddenly exclaimed. "Adriana?" Powell hadn't seen Afina's little sister for about three years. She had been sixteen when he rescued her from the sex traffickers.

"Have I changed so much?"

Powell stood up and kissed Adriana on each cheek.

Afina was smiling. "Now you see why I was laughing."

Powell felt a pang of guilt for how he had been eyeing Adriana. "I really didn't recognise you. You look so different. You changed the colour of your hair. And you grew about three inches!"

"Do you like me as a redhead?"

"It looks great. When did you arrive?"

"Two days ago."

"Afina, you should have told me Adriana was coming."

"I wanted to surprise you. She is staying for the Summer and then she goes to university."

"Well it's great to see you again, Adriana. And your English is excellent."

"Thank you but it is not so good. It is the reason I come to England. I must practice. Now, I better get back to work. I have a very tough boss."

"I'm really not tough," Powell replied.

"I meant Afina," Adriana explained with a broad smile.

"We'll catch up soon," Powell promised.

When Adriana was out of earshot, Afina asked, "I hope you don't mind my recruiting my sister?"

"Of course not. It's great to see her again. Was your mother okay with her coming to England?"

"She is happy Adriana is staying with me and working in your bar. She thinks you are a very special man."

"I like your mother. She is obviously a good judge of character."

"She may change her opinion when I tell her how you look at her youngest daughter."

"I've often looked the same way at her eldest daughter," Powell joked. It wasn't really true anymore. That Powell loved Afina wasn't in doubt but she had become more of a surrogate daughter than a potential lover. It hadn't always been the case and he sometimes questioned his sanity as she had made it clear she wanted a relationship. He used their age difference to justify his decision but it wasn't the real reason. He was dangerous to be around. Both his wife and daughter had been murdered. He couldn't face the same happening to Afina so he tried to keep her at a safe distance.

Afina was lost for words for a moment. "I think it has been a long time since you looked at me like that."

"Not true but I try to be discrete," Powell replied lightheartedly.

"I need to get back to work," Afina said, rising from her chair.

"We must all go out sometime soon," Powell suggested. "That is if Adriana's tough boss will allow her some time off."

"I'll arrange something," Afina confirmed and started to walk away. After a few steps she turned suddenly. She caught Powell staring in her direction. She smiled and continued on her way.

Powell felt a little foolish but his thoughts were interrupted by his phone ringing.

"Hello, Angela," he answered.

"Powell. Can you come up to London urgently. It's Rose. She's in a terrible way. She needs help."

"Slow down. What's happened to Rose?"

"Her bloody husband has beaten her up."

Powell was shocked. "Did she tell him what she discovered?"

"She says she fell down the stairs. But I don't believe her. I popped around this morning for a coffee and I almost had to force my way in the house. She didn't want me to see her looking like that. If it had been an accident, she wouldn't have minded. I'm sure it's him."

"How is she?"

"Black eyes and a broken nose. And that's just the injuries I can see!"

"What do you want me to do?"

"We need to go pay her a visit."

Powell knew he had to find out if Rose had alerted her husband to the discovery of the speech. She may even have mentioned his name while being beaten up. If that was the case, he certainly didn't blame Rose, he just needed to know, because if she had, it was inevitable there would be repercussions.

"I can meet you at Rose's at two thirty," Powell suggested.

"Thank you, Powell."

CHAPTER EIGHT

Powell took a taxi from Victoria station to the coffee shop at the end of the street where Rose lived. Angela was waiting inside, hovering close to the door. He hadn't wanted her hanging around on the pavement outside Rose's house.

"Do you want a coffee?" Powell asked.

"Rose will make us coffee," Angela answered impatiently.

"Let's go then," he replied, holding the door open for Angela.

It was a two minute walk to Rose's house. Powell searched the Mews for signs of anything out of place. There was a BT van parked a few doors down from the house but otherwise there was no discernible signs of life. The Mews was an expensive oasis of calm in the centre of London.

Powell stood to the side of the door as Angela rang the bell. It was half opened by Rose and then seeing Angela on the doorstep, the door was fully opened.

Powell stepped forward into view. "We need to talk," he said.

Rose was flustered by his sudden appearance. "Really, Angela. You can't keep turning up uninvited. I just had an accident. I don't need your or Powell's help."

"Let's talk inside," Powell suggested and didn't give Rose a chance to object further as he stepped inside the house.

"I'm not a child," Rose protested. "If I need help, I'll ask for it."

Angela followed Powell through the doorway and closed the door behind them.

Powell had the opportunity to study Rose's injuries for the first time. She looked like she had gone ten rounds with a boxer.

"So you fell down the stairs?" Powell queried.

"It was just a stupid accident," Rose replied but she avoided eye contact with Powell.

"Why don't you two go in the lounge," Angela encouraged. "I'll make us some coffee."

Rose didn't argue further and led the way into the living room.

"Sorry about barging in," Powell said once seated. "Angela's concerned for you."

Rose managed a weak smile. "She's a good friend. But she really doesn't like George. It's not his fault I had an accident."

"So you haven't said anything to him about the speech?"

"Of course not," Rose replied quickly, looking down at the floor.

Powell wasn't convinced. "Rose, your husband is associating with ruthless men. They appear to have carried out an act of terrorism with total disregard for the loss of life. Whatever your husband has said to you, if he knows you have seen the speech, your life is in danger."

"Powell, I know you mean well. George isn't perfect but I'm the mother of his children. He wouldn't do anything to put my life in danger."

"It may not be his decision to make."

Angela entered carrying three mugs of coffee. "You should listen to Powell," she advised firmly, handing Rose her coffee. "He knows what he's talking about."

"Can we please change the subject," Rose implored. "I fell down the stairs. That's the end of the matter."

"Can I take another look at your husband's computer?" Powell requested. "I want to see if there have been anymore emails from the Chairman."

"He's changed the password," Rose answered and yet again avoided Powell's gaze.

"When did that happen?" Powell probed.

"I don't know. It could have been anytime," Rose answered angrily. "I don't monitor what he does every minute of the day."

"So when did you find out it was changed?"

"I..." Rose hesitated. "I tried looking yesterday and it was changed."

Powell was now certain Rose was lying. "Do you think he suspects you had been looking at his computer?"

"No. I don't know why he changed his bloody password." Rose stood up. "Now I'd like you both to leave. I need to rest not be cross examined like I'm on trial for something."

"Sorry," Angela apologised. "We're just trying to help." She took Rose's hands in her own. "I know George did this to you. Why don't you tell Powell the truth? Then he can help you."

"What's he going to do? He can't protect all of us."

"What do you mean, *protect all of us*?" Powell questioned. "Who has he threatened?"

"Please just go," Rose pleaded. "The children will be back soon from school. I don't want them to see you here."

"Why don't you want the children to see us?" Angela quizzed "You are always telling me how much they like me."

"I'm trying to protect you," Rose answered. "George warned me not to speak to anyone. If the children tell him you were here…"

"I'm not afraid of your husband," Angela said defiantly. "And neither should you be. Why do you stay with him?"

"Leaving isn't so easy. I don't have any money of my own and he would ensure I never get to see my children."

"What nonsense," Angela responded. "Take the children with you."

"He'd never let me do that."

"You aren't going to ask for his permission," Angela stated. "You can all come and stay with me until you get yourself sorted."

Rose seemed to consider the idea for a moment then her shoulders sagged and she responded, "We can't do that. The kids have to go to school. If I ever left George, I would have to leave the country."

"Not if you report him to the police for assault," Angela encouraged. "You could get a restraining order and he wouldn't dare try anything then."

"It's not that simple. He would deny everything and he has friends in high places."

"Have you thought about getting a divorce?" Powell asked.

"George says, he will prove I'm an unfit mother and win sole custody of the children, if I ever try to leave him."

"I'd like to see him try," Angela replied. "You're a fabulous mother."

"So Rose, I think it's time you told us the truth about your injuries," Powell said gently.

Rose sunk into an armchair. "He came home early last night. Actually, he stopped by to collect some papers he needed for a meeting. I didn't hear him come in and when he walked into the study, I was on his computer. He went ballistic."

"Why didn't you call the police?" Angela asked.

"He said it was my fault he lost his temper. If I hadn't been snooping he wouldn't have hurt me.

"How dare he blame you!" Angela explained. "What did they say at the hospital?"

"I never went. George said there would be too many awkward questions for a man in his position if I went to the hospital."

"And you listened to him?" Angela asked in disbelief.

"I didn't have much choice. After he found me in the study, he dragged me up to the bedroom. He kept hitting me and then he… After he'd finished, he warned me if I didn't do exactly as he instructed, he knew men who liked to play rough with women."

"Dear God, Rose!" Angela exclaimed. "You can't stay with this monster." Angela put her arms around Rose for a hug and Rose winced in pain. Angela quickly let go. "Has he broken any ribs?"

"No. I'm just bruised," Rose explained.

"We need to call the police and take you to hospital," Angela said.

"I'm so scared," Rose admitted, bursting into tears.

"You're safe now," Angela replied, gripping Rose's hand tightly. "We won't let him hurt you again."

After a minute Rose composed herself and stepped back. She managed a weak smile. "It's all my fault. I shouldn't have been prying into his affairs. He's honestly not a bad man. He's never done anything like this before."

"Don't make excuses for him," Angela replied forcefully. "You always said you were prone to accidents and I believed you, but now I know the truth. This isn't the first time he's hit you."

"His work is very stressful. Sometimes I mess up and he loses his temper. He's always sorry the next day."

Angela nodded her head with a look of disbelief.

Powell had been observing so far, allowing Angela the chance to get to the truth. She had done a good job of getting Rose to admit she had been beaten up by her husband. "Rose, I have to ask. Did you tell George we know about the speech?" Powell probed.

"No. I said I thought he was having an affair. That was the truth. He assumed it was the first time I'd been on his laptop."

"Does he even know you've seen the speech?" Powell enquired.

"I had it open on his laptop when he entered."

"I think we should get you out of here," Powell said firmly.

"I can't just leave. It's too dangerous."

"It might be more dangerous to do nothing," Powell suggested. "I don't know exactly what your husband has got himself involved with but the stakes are obviously extremely high. If he tells the people behind the terrorist attack that you know about the speech, they are bound to be very nervous. In their place, I would sleep a lot better with you out of the way."

"You mean, you think they will try and kill me?" Rose looked visibly shaken by the idea.

"I don't think you should wait around to find out. After all, they have already proved they have a callous disregard for human life."

"Please listen to Powell," Angela stressed.

Before Rose could answer, the doorbell rang. She seemed reluctant to move and whoever was outside rang the bell a second time.

"Do you want me to go?" Powell asked.

"It's probably better I go," Angela suggested, rising from her chair. Powell tried to give Rose a reassuring smile as he also stood up and moved to stand behind the lounge door. It seemed an unnecessary precaution but he'd rather err on the side of caution. He could hear a male voice on the doorstep followed by Angela's voice.

Powell moved to the bay window and pulled back the net curtain. There were two men in suits at the front door. Powell had a phobia about men in dark suits. In his experience, they always brought trouble. He watched as the two men walked away from the house. One man put his phone to his ear.

Angela reappeared.

"What did they want?" Powell asked, still staring out of the window.

"They were from BT. They are going to be digging up the road next week and wanted to let everyone know."

"What are you looking at?" Rose enquired.

Powell saw the man finish his phone call and then he said something to his colleague. They looked back in the direction of the house. Powell let go of the curtain.

"Is there a back way out of here?" Powell questioned.

"Why?" Angela asked. "Is there something wrong?"

"I don't think they are from BT. They are only interested in this house. Rose, can we get out through the rear?"

"No," Rose answered. "What should we do?"

The doorbell rang again.

"I'll get it," Powell announced. "They won't be expecting to see me. Rose, call the police right now and say two men are trying to break into your house. Act terrified."

"I don't have to act."

The doorbell rang again twice more in quick succession. The men outside were getting impatient.

Powell waited until he heard Rose being connected with the police and start to give her address. Then he walked to the front door. He was pleased the door was made of wood and very solid. He slid the door chain in place and opened the door a few inches.

"Can I help you?" Powell asked.

The two men couldn't keep the surprise from their faces. They hadn't expected to find a man answering the door.

"Hello, Sir. We are from BT. We were just talking to a woman. Was she your wife?" The man who spoke had a square jaw and a serious expression.

"I'm not married," Powell stated abruptly. He was convinced they didn't work for BT. They looked more like Undertakers.

"Can we come in a minute? We have a few further questions."

"Sorry," Powell replied. "Can you come back another time, only it really isn't convenient right now."

Powell could see indecision in the man's eyes. There wasn't supposed to be a man in the house. They had probably been led to believe only Rose would be at home. When they found Angela answering the door, they had telephoned for instructions. Powell reckoned the orders had been to take out both women. Now he was providing a further complication.

He took his phone from his pocket and took several pictures through the gap in the door. Then he slammed the door shut just as the men on the other side started to protest.

CHAPTER NINE

Powell returned to the living room and once again peered through the net curtains. The two men were standing on the pavement and a further phone call was being made. Powell would have loved to know who was on the other end of the phone. Was it George Carter?

Powell turned back and looked at Rose. "Get some clothes together. We're leaving in a few minutes and I don't think you will be coming back anytime soon."

"What about the children?" Rose asked. "I'm going nowhere without them."

"What time do they finish school?"

Rose looked at her watch. "They both do dance tonight so will be finished in about an hour."

"We'll go collect them as soon as we get rid of the two men out front."

"Where are we going?" Rose asked.

"You can all come stay with me," Angela volunteered.

"That's the first place they will look," Powell replied. "And it's best you don't know where to find Rose. Then you don't have to lie if someone does ask."

Powell glanced back out the window just as a police car pulled up outside. The two men in suits started to walk away but the two police officers quickly approached them and engaged in a conversation. After a couple of minutes it was obvious an argument was developing.

Powell wanted to warn the police officers the men were dangerous but even as the thought crossed his mind, the two men attacked the officers. In a blur of movement both policemen were knocked to the ground. The two assailants then ran to the BT van and there was a screech of tyres as they pulled away.

Powell hurried outside to check on the policemen. One was unconscious but the other was trying to climb to his feet. Powell helped him up and opening the car door, sat him sideways on the passenger seat with his feet on the ground.

Powell bent over the officer on the ground and turned him on his side into the recovery position. Meanwhile the officer in the car called for assistance and an ambulance. Powell stood back up and gave him the registration number of the BT van.

Rose and Angela had followed Powell out of the house and were standing close by, uncertain what to do.

"Rose, go get started on that packing," Powell instructed. "Angela, go make some tea."

Two police cars with sirens blaring arrived and officers spilled out. One of the officers approached Powell, while the others saw to their colleagues.

"Did you see what happened?" the officer questioned.

"Two men in dark suits, who said they were from BT, tried to get into Rose Carter's house. She is the wife of George Carter, the MP." The officer raised his eyebrows. Powell pointed towards the house. "She lives there. I was visiting at the time with another friend, Angela Bennett. I thought the men were suspicious and closed the door on them. Mrs Carter then called the police. When your men arrived they questioned the two suspects. Then the men suddenly attacked your officers before making off in a van, which said BT on the side. I gave the registration number to your colleague."

"And your name, Sir?"

"Powell."

"Would you recognise these men if you saw them again?"

The noise of an ambulance's siren entering the mews was so overwhelming, Powell didn't try and reply. Everyone had to clear a path to allow it closer access to the injured.

"I'm not sure if I could recognise them," Powell answered once the ambulance was quiet. "I only had a quick look at them. They were both just average height, slim, mid-thirties." Powell wasn't going to reveal he had taken pictures on his phone or he would never see his phone again. "There was nothing very distinguishing about them. They were wearing blue suits and had short hair. You know who they really looked like?"

"Who?" The policeman dutifully prompted.

"They looked like FBI men always look in the movies."

The policeman sighed and put his notebook way. "Thanks for your help. If you do remember anything a little more specific, please don't hesitate to get in touch."

As Powell had provided his contact details, he was allowed back in the house, which wasn't considered a crime scene.

Angela and Rose were interviewed but had nothing to add to Powell's brief statement. Rose pointed out there was a CCTV camera at the entrance to the mews, which quickly became the focus of attention for the officers.

"We should get going," Powell suggested, once the police had left them alone. He was concerned Rose's husband would turn up and complicate matters.

"Do you know where you are going?" Angela asked.

"It's all arranged. I made a call while you were upstairs helping Rose pack."

"Are you going to be staying with Rose?" Angela enquired.

"No. I will just see she is safe and then return to Brighton. I need to find some answers." Powell didn't want to explain to Angela that he was going to be the bait to find those answers. He expected someone to come after him in an attempt to find Rose. He wouldn't be difficult for professionals to track down. His name was now part of the official police record of the incident. "You won't be able to speak to Rose for a few days. For her safety, she needs to be completely cut off from the world."

"I understand."

"Speaking of which," Powell said, turning to Rose. "You need to leave your phone behind."

"Can't I just turn it off?"

"No. They can trace it even when it's off. When we leave here, we will find a cash machine and you can withdraw as much money as you are allowed from all your cards. Then you must not use them again. You won't need much money where you are going."

Rose didn't look convinced but didn't argue. "We better get going. The children will be out of school shortly."

"Angela, you should head off home." Powell suggested. "I will call you when I get back to Brighton."

CHAPTER TEN

Powell hadn't had much time to think of somewhere safe for Rose and the children to hide. Brighton was out of the question. In spy parlance, he needed a safe house. Somewhere the family could take refuge from the danger they were facing. In other circumstances, Powell might have asked Brian for access to an MI5 safe house but not on this occasion. Anything linked to the institutions of government couldn't be guaranteed to be safe.

Powell knew only one person who spent his life trying to stay hidden from the rest of the world. Samurai was a professional hacker, sometimes working for the government and often not. Whoever he was working for, what he did was rarely legal. He had helped Powell on a couple of previous occasions. Although his services didn't come cheap, he was always overloaded with work. Unfortunately, he was in a line of work where he continually made enemies. As a result, moving home was a regular occurrence.

Powell couldn't really say he either liked or disliked Samurai. He was a geek, who preferred to interact with computers rather than humans. Despite his lack of social skills, Powell certainly respected Samurai's technical skills. He hadn't so much boasted as stated factually that given enough time, he could access any system.

He had been offered large sums of money to work exclusively for criminal organisations but refused as he preferred a variety of challenges in his work. Powell also suspected that under the indifferent attitude lurked someone who enjoyed sometimes being on the side of the good guys.

Powell called Tina, who was Samurai's sister, despite no two people ever having been more different. There had been an attraction on both sides in the past but it had never been given the chance to develop. He hadn't visited her new home in the Midlands but knew it was a large property with extensive grounds. Tina quickly agreed to help and suggested Rose and the children could have the flat above the garage. Tina lived quite a secluded life and seemed to welcome the idea of visitors.

Before leaving the house, Powell had Rose send a text to her husband. She told him she wanted a divorce and was going away for a few days with the kids. She hadn't told Angela or anyone in her family where she was going so don't bother looking. Within a minute of sending the message, her husband called but she didn't answer. George didn't like being ignored and there were several angry voicemails before Rose left the phone on the table.

After meeting the children from school, Rose told them they were going away for a few days of surprise holiday. Being eleven and ten years old, Simon and Imogen were full of questions about where they were going and for how long, but they were completely unconcerned their father was too busy to go with them.

They all took a train to Nottingham, which peeked the children's interest as they enquired about Robin Hood. Otherwise, the only time the children took their eyes away from their top of the range iPhones, was when Rose offered drinks and crisps. Powell suspected the children had a very different upbringing to that which he had provided his daughter. Mobile phones hadn't existed and even watching television was limited. Playing was something you did outside with friends not on an electronic device.

They were met at Nottingham station by Tina and twenty five minutes later they reached their destination. The secluded house was impressive as were the security measures. The large wall was interrupted by an entrance with electronic gates and an intercom system. Cameras perched on the wall above the sides of the gate. Powell felt confident the family would be safe within the confines of the walls. The grounds would also allow the children room to explore without feeling prisoners.

Powell joined Samurai and Tina in the office while Rose and the children unpacked. He recounted the events of the last few days.

"That's terrible," Tina commented. "I'm going to go see if Rose needs anything."

"Do you want me to look into this Chairman and his friends?" Samurai asked after Tina had left.

"Yes, please."

"I don't want paying. It's been too long since I did some pro bono work for a good cause."

"Thanks."

"It won't be easy. I'd normally start with his email account but if he's using Protonmail then that's a dead end."

"I thought you could access any email system?"

"Generally true but Protonmail was developed by some very clever people to be completely secure."

"Do your best. That's always been good enough in the past."

"What are you going to do?"

"I'm going to head back to Brighton. I expect them to come looking for me."

Samurai was thoughtful for a moment. "If they find you, they will make you tell them where to find the wife and kids. Then we will all become targets. I don't mind the risk for myself but Tina…"

Powell couldn't argue with Samurai's logic. It was the most words Powell had ever heard him string together in one sentence. Powell didn't want to dwell on what someone would have to do to him to make him reveal the family's whereabouts. That he could be broken, he had no doubt. It was impossible to remain silent when someone attacked your body with a blow torch.

"There is always that risk," Powell agreed. "If you don't want them here, I'll make other arrangements."

"I didn't say we wouldn't help. I'm just wondering if we should hire some extra security?"

"That may not be such a bad idea. Let me speak with Jenkins and see if he is available." Jenkins had helped Powell out of a number of tight spots over recent times. He was a tough and reliable former soldier. Exactly what was currently needed. He had also previously met Samurai and Tina.

"Jenkins would be a good solution," Samurai agreed. "Tina likes him as well."

"Great. I'll call him straight away."

CHAPTER ELEVEN

Powell had declined the offer to stay the night and instead took a late train back to Brighton. Before leaving he spoke to Jenkins, who was going to head off to Nottingham first thing in the morning. Samurai and Tina knew Jenkins and were pleased that it would be a familiar face providing the extra security.

Brian had poked around in the dark corners of the intelligence service but discovered nothing of value. His next logical step would be to speak with the Director General but with no real evidence to back up what would sound like wild accusations, they had decided to hold off on that step for the time being.

Back home, Powell stepped into his hallway, pulling the front door closed. As always, he felt a sense of calm. His home was a quiet oasis from the noise of the bar. As was his routine, he hung his jacket on the wall beside the door and reached for the light switch. He silently cursed the lack of light and another defunct bulb.

He turned towards the kitchen where he kept spare bulbs and that was when he heard the creak. He had no pets and after living so long in the house, he knew there could be only one explanation for the noise. He was certain it was the sound of someone shifting his weight from one foot to the other. The floorboards never lied and the broken lightbulb was further evidence he had an intruder.

The sound had come behind the lounge door on his left. Someone was waiting for him on the other side of the door. Maybe more than one person. He walked towards the kitchen where at least there were some large knives for defence, although regrettably he didn't keep a gun in the house.

Powell heard a further creak behind him as a figure rushed forward. He spun around ready to confront the danger. The assailant was bringing a baseball bat down in a vicious arc towards his back. Powell twisted his body out of the way and without hesitation delivered a kick to the groin, which caused his attacker to cry out and bend double.

The bat fell to the ground as Powell saw a further man emerge from behind his partner. There was little room to manoeuvre in the narrow hallway. The attacker pushed past his struggling colleague, swinging a punch towards Powell's chin. The wild swing missed and Powell delivered a short jab to the man's throat, which left him desperately gasping for air. In his panic, he took a step backwards and fell over his friend.

The first man tried to climb to his feet and Powell kicked him hard in the head.

"Stay down," Powell warned. He was feeling more relaxed as the two men were certainly not the most professional he'd ever faced. They also weren't here to kill him armed with a bat and fists.

Both men were slumped on the ground. In the gloomy darkness they were little more than shadows but Powell could distinguish that one was tall and the other quite short.

Powell picked up the baseball bat. He held it above his head and made a gesture as if he was going to strike. The tall man clutching his throat whimpered and raised his arms for protection. The other man seemed to be out cold.

Powell took a step backwards and opened the door to his downstairs toilet. He switched on the light, which enabled him to get a better view of the two assailants on the floor. They were young, probably both in their mid-twenties and had more than their fair share of both tattoos and muscles. Powell guessed they spent many hours in a gym lifting weights. Their time would have been better spent learning fighting skills.

They weren't the same men who had earlier attacked the police officers outside Rose's home. Powell was happy to see the one who was conscious looking scared.

"If you want to walk out of here rather than be taken away in an ambulance, you need to answer my questions," Powell threatened. "I will know if you are lying and there will be no second warnings. Every time I think you aren't telling the truth or you are too slow answering, I will break a bone in your body."

"Fuck you!" the man replied and tried to stand up.

Powell hit him on the back of one calf causing him to collapse to the floor, swearing loudly.

"I warned you," Powell said after a moment. "Next time I will aim for your shin and break your leg." He didn't expect any further resistance.

The second man on the floor stirred. He raised his head off the ground.

"Sit up," Powell instructed. "Both of you sit with your backs against the wall. Powell waved the bat a little to encourage them to move quicker and slowly the men dragged their battered bodies into position.

"As I was saying," Powell continued. "You will answer my questions. Who sent you?"

Neither man hurried to answer.

Powell raised the baseball bat over his head. His intention seemed obvious. However, while both men looked to the bat, Powell lashed out with his leg and landed a kick flush to the jaw of the nearest man, who had only just regained consciousness. The blow was controlled and only half power. It sent the man's head spinning backwards against the wall.

"Did I not make myself clear?" Powell demanded. "Who sent you?"

This time the man who had just been kicked in the head answered quickly. "We don't really know. I mean, it's just someone at the end of the phone."

"What were your instructions?"

"He told us he needed the answer to some questions. We were to make you secure and then call him back. He was then going to tell us what questions to ask."

"Seems like we have a bit of a role reversal. I don't suppose I would have liked how you asked the questions. What did he tell you about me?"

"Nothing. He just said that it would be an easy way to earn some quick money."

Once again Powell gave thanks the opposition had underestimated his skills and sent boys to do a man's job. They must have assumed he was just an untrained and interfering old friend of Rose.

"Give me your phone," Powell demanded, holding out his hand.

The man passed over his phone without argument. "What are you going to do with us?" he asked.

It was a good question. "What is your contact's number?" Powell asked. Once he had the number, he telephoned Brian and asked him to trace the owner of the phone.

"How were you going to get paid?" Powell asked, turning back to the two men.

"I gave him our bank details. He paid half up front and the rest we get after."

"I don't think you'll be getting that second payment," Powell smiled. "What was I worth?"

"A grand to each of us."

Powell felt undervalued. "Give me your wallets," he demanded.

Both men hesitated. Powell gave the nearest a kick in the shin, which did the trick. Powell opened the first wallet and found a bank card. "Is this the account?"

"Yes."

He did the same with the second wallet and received the same positive response.

"Okay so let me explain what happens next. You two have inadvertently got mixed up in something far bigger than you realise. I am going to let you both go but I am going to keep your wallets. If I never hear from you again, you won't hear from me. However, I have friends in high places, who owe me many favours and I am going to pass them your details. If anything should happen to me, they will find you and put an end to your miserable lives. I would recommend you both disappear for some time. The people who hired you are going to feel let down and might not be as forgiving as me."

Both men shook their heads vigorously in agreement.

"Do you have transport?" Powell queried.

"Car's parked down the road," the taller man answered.

"Then why are you still sitting here?"

CHAPTER TWELVE

Powell watched the two men drive away and then hurriedly threw a few clothes and his toothbrush into an overnight bag. He had decided it probably wasn't safe to stay at the house but more importantly he was in need of some sleep. He doubted the two men would be foolish enough to return but he knew if he stayed in the house, he wouldn't get any sleep thinking about the possibility.

Before leaving, Powell called Brian and gave him the bank details he had obtained from the two attackers. Hopefully, Brian would be able to trace the account from which five hundred pounds had been paid to each man. Between the phone number he provided earlier and the bank account, Powell hoped Brian would be able to shed some light on who was involved. It would probably only be a middle man carrying out orders but at least it was somewhere to start.

Before driving to the bar, Powell phoned Afina to ask if she would mind him sleeping on the sofa in her lounge. Despite owning the bar and the flat above, where Afina lived, he would never assume he could just turn up. It was Afina's home and her decision whether he could stay. He knew the answer would be affirmative but one day he would like to hear that it wasn't convenient because she had a boyfriend staying over.

In any event, he would still visit the bar because it was where he kept a gun locked away in the safe, in his office. He intended to keep the weapon very close to his person over the next few days. When they came for him the next time, he expected them to be armed. That there would be a second time, he had no doubt.

It was after midnight when Powell arrived at the bar. It had just closed and Afina was in the process of saying good night to the staff. He poured himself a whisky and sat himself on a stool waiting for everyone to leave. After about five minutes the last of the staff had left. Afina helped herself to a bottle of Coke from behind the bar and joined him on the next stool.

"Busy night?" Powell asked.

"About average."

"Thanks for letting me use the sofa tonight."

"That's all right. Adriana can sleep with me tonight."

Powell had forgotten all about Afina's younger sister. "I'm sorry. I should have known she would be occupying the sofa. Do you want me to check into a hotel?"

"It's not a problem. She went up to bed just before you arrived. She's finding it hard work."

"You're not working her extra hard because she's your sister?" Powell queried.

"No. She wants to work double shifts to make extra money."

"She is driven, just like you."

"What does *driven* mean?"

Powell thought about it for a second. "Ambitious."

"Maybe. But she is cleverer than me. She is going to university."

"We all walk different paths in life."

"My path has not been very straight," Afina smiled.

"Neither has mine. I have always believed attitude is more important than qualifications."

"So what is wrong with your house?" Afina suddenly asked. "Are you in trouble?"

Powell realised he should have prepared an answer. Afina always said what she was thinking. "No. I'm not in trouble. I was burgled while I was away and I don't want to clear up the mess until the morning."

"Who were these burglars? And what did they want?"

"Afina, I have no idea. They were just burglars."

"What did they steal?"

"Nothing important."

"They must be a new kind of burglar. They break into houses but take nothing important. Or perhaps they are apprentices like Stuart in the kitchen, learning on the job."

"I'm not sure what they've taken. I'll check in the morning. I was too tired tonight."

Afina raised her eyebrows, indicating she didn't believe his explanation for a second. "Have you reported this to the police?"

"Not yet."

"So you rush off to London to meet Angela and then your house is burgled but you don't bother to inform the police. I'm not stupid, Powell and I've known you too long. Why won't you simply be honest with me?"

"Because I don't want you getting involved."

"That must be because you believe telling me would put me in danger."

"There is that possibility," Powell admitted.

"Please don't bring any danger to the bar," Afina said seriously. "Not with Adriana here."

"It's just one night," Powell promised.

The Chairman listened to the man on the other end of the phone with a growing sense of horror. Was he working with complete imbeciles? First, George Carter had been dangerously foolish and now the man at the end of the phone had compounded the problem by his inept attempts to silence Carter's wife. The police were even involved.

"There's more," the man said, although he hated having to share further bad news with the Chairman. "I had two men pay a visit to this Powell's home to find out the wife's whereabouts. They seem to have disappeared."

"Perhaps you hired magicians by mistake. Who did you use for the job?"

"They were local help I haven't used before."

"Why didn't you use the same men as at the house? They have been very efficient in the past."

"I thought they should lie low after what happened at Carter's house. They attacked two police officers."

"So what are you going to do about this Powell?"

"We'll find him tomorrow and this time there won't be any mistakes."

"I hope not. Use whatever resources you deem necessary but get this fixed. The next call I receive from you better be to tell me the problem has gone away. Do I make myself clear?"

"Very clear."

The Chairman ended the call and then scanned his list of contacts. He found the number he wanted and when the voice answered, he simply instructed the man at the other end of the phone to be on the next plane to England.

The Chairman knew he was over reacting but he was buying himself some extra insurance. The Irishman was one hundred per cent reliable. It would mean a small delay in his plans to increase the President's popularity but the Irishman should complete the job and be back within a couple of weeks at the most. The President could stay healthy but unloved for a little longer. The Chairman wasn't going to entrust the shooting of the President to anyone but the Irishman.

CHAPTER THIRTEEN

Tina enjoyed having some female company in the house for a change. She had stayed up late with Rose, chatting and drinking wine. Tina had been unable to keep pace with Rose, who consumed a bottle of Prosecco in less than an hour. Tina assumed it was a reaction to everything Rose had gone through recently. The more wine Rose consumed, the more open she was about her husband. The bruises on her face were beginning to fade but she revealed her husband had always had a vile temper and quick fists. Although Tina couldn't comprehend why anyone would stay with such a man, she wasn't too critical. Rose needed someone to listen not pass judgement.

Speaking to Rose made Tina reflect on her own life. She was generally happy with the way of life she had chosen and recognised she lived a privileged if sometimes lonely existence. Financial security had given her independence but it was difficult to make true friends, when her brother's work regularly dictated the need to move house. She felt very protective towards her brother. He was a brilliant computer geek but she sometimes wondered if he suffered from a mild form of Asperger's. Certainly, he would struggle if she ever moved out.

Rose helped prepare breakfast for the children, who were excited by their new surroundings. Tina was slightly surprised Rose showed no signs of a hangover. It was the first time in a long while, Tina could remember sitting around a table enjoying a family meal. Her brother took his meals in the office and she was accustomed to more of the than not eating alone.

The entry system announced someone was at the gate and Tina looked at the CCTV to check who was buzzing. She was surprised and concerned to see two vehicles trying to gain access. They looked as if they were on official business. She wanted to believe Powell had arranged some additional security but knew that was highly unlikely as he would have said something.

"Hello," Tina spoke into the intercom. "How can I help you?"

A man's voice replied. "This is Detective Inspector Sharpe. We have a search warrant for this property."

"What are you searching for?"

"Please open the gate," the Inspector demanded.

"Just a moment," Tina replied. She turned to Rose. "Take the children and go to the safe room, I showed you."

"What's wrong?" Rose asked, suddenly worried. "Is it my husband?"

"Just go to the safe room and lock yourselves inside. It's just a precaution. We have a visit from the police."

Tina tried to give Rose an encouraging smile as she nervously ushered the children out of the kitchen. Tina then spoke into the phone again. "Inspector, I need to verify you really are a police officer? Only you really can't be too careful nowadays. One hears about so many fraudsters conning their way into houses. I am just going to call 999 and then I will be right back."

Tina didn't wait to hear the Inspector's reply. She hurried to the office and informed her brother the police were at the gate. It was quite possible the police were more interested in his activities than the presence of Rose and her children.

He immediately hit a key on his computer that initiated automatic processes, which removed evidence of his work. There was no actual data stored on the computer but he still hid it in a cleverly concealed space in the wall. He put a different computer, he kept especially for the purpose, on his desk so it didn't look as if the original one was missing. It was a routine they had practiced on a number of occasions.

Tina called 999 and after a few minutes, the friendly operator confirmed that the man at the gate really was Detective Inspector Sharpe with a search warrant.

Tina returned to the entry phone. "Please could you hold up your identification to the camera."

The Inspector took his warrant card from his pocket and held it up in front of the camera mounted at the side of the gate. "Satisfied?" he demanded.

"That seems in order," Tina replied. She was aware the officer was becoming very impatient. "I'm opening the gate now."

Tina opened the front door and watched the two cars come up the drive and park in front of the house.

DI Sharpe stepped out of the first car. He was wearing a blue suit, which had seen better days. Tina assessed him to be in his mid-thirties. He wasn't very tall but not particularly short. Everything about him fitted the definition of average. His expression suggested he would have preferred to be somewhere else.

The DI was accompanied by a police woman in uniform, who looked very young. They were joined from the second car by a woman dressed in a grey trouser suit. Tina's instincts told her the visit was related to Rose and the children.

"I'm DI Sharpe," the man in the suit confirmed unnecessarily. He indicated each of the others in turn as he made introductions. "This is Officer Hartley and Jane Price from Social Services."

Tina made no attempt to shake hands or appear overly welcoming. "Let's go inside," she said and led the way into the hall.

Once inside, DI Sharpe came quickly to the point. "Are Rose Carter and her two children here?"

"Why do you ask?" Tina responded.

"I'll ask the questions," DI Sharpe said bluntly. "We know the children are here. Please take us to them."

Tina was wondering how the police had discovered the whereabouts of the children. "Detective Inspector, Rose and the children have been through a terrible ordeal. They are here to rest and recover. Why does that interest the police?"

"That is not your business. If you do not take me to them I will have you arrested."

"And why are Social Services here?" Tina added, ignoring the threat.

"Are you going to take me to them?" DI Sharpe demanded.

"It isn't as simple as that. Rose Carter and her children are in a secure room in the house. It can only be opened from the inside."

"What do you mean by a secure room?" DI Sharpe asked, a little taken aback.

"We have what is usually referred to as a safe room."

"May I ask why you need such a room?"

"You may…"

"Well?"

"I said you could ask, not that I would answer."

"How do I speak with Mrs. Carter?" DI Sharpe asked, obviously irritated.

"She has seen and heard everything since you arrived," Tina replied. "We have CCTV in every room in the house and it feeds back to the safe room."

DI Sharpe seemed momentarily confused by the revelation. He cast his eyes around the hall until he spotted the camera, high up on the wall in one corner.

"Mrs. Carter," DI Sharpe said out loud, looking in the direction of the camera. "Will you please come down here."

"Is Rose being arrested?" Tina interrupted.

"Not at this time."

"Then she doesn't have to speak to you?"

"If she doesn't come down here, I will be left with no choice but to arrest her."

"On what charge?"

"We have cause to believe Mrs. Carter has abducted her children and presents a potential threat to their welfare."

"What rubbish!" Tina exclaimed. "The children are perfectly safe here."

The social Services woman spoke for the first time. "Mrs. Carter has taken the children out of school and brought them here without saying anything to her husband, who is obviously very concerned about her erratic behaviour. It's fortunate both the children have GPS tracking devices in their necklaces. From what I can see, we have every right to be concerned about the children's welfare."

Tina knew it was wrong to make such a fast judgement but she didn't like the woman from Social Services. "Of course she hasn't said anything to her husband. She is black and blue with bruises sustained from his fists." Tina noticed the surprised glance exchanged between DI Sharpe and his colleague. "Rose Carter is afraid for her life and didn't want her husband to know where she is staying."

"Perhaps Mrs. Carter would care to come down and show us these bruises?" DI Sharpe interjected, once again staring up towards the camera.

"Will you then leave?" Tina quickly queried. She suspected the police officer's interest in Rose's bruises was simply a ploy to draw the family out of the safe room.

DI Sharpe looked towards Jane Price and raised his eyebrows.

"I am purely concerned with the welfare of the children," Jane Price reiterated. "They shouldn't be missing school. If the mother wishes to make a complaint to the police about her husband, that is an entirely separate matter."

Tina made a point of looking only at DI Sharpe. "Is it normal for the police to hunt down children after missing one day of school? Not to mention, treat their mother as a criminal for escaping an abusive husband?"

DI Sharpe looked uncomfortable for the first time since he arrived. "My role here is to ensure Social Services have access to the children so they can determine what is best for the children."

"And you think this woman, who has never met Rose or her children is best placed to decide what is best for these children? Do you have children, Detective Inspector?"

"If Mrs. Carter would just come down then I'm sure we can quickly resolve this matter."

"My problem, Detective Inspector, is that the very appearance of someone from Social Services accompanied by yourself, makes me question what exactly is going on here. Mr. Carter is an influential man and I suspect this woman arrived here fully intending to take the children back to London, with or without their mother's consent."

"I'm sure that's not…" DI Sharpe started to answer.

"We have received reports that give us cause for concern about the mental state of Mrs. Carter," Jane Price interrupted. "We are going to place the children with their father while we investigate further."

"I bet one guess would be sufficient to know who made these unfounded allegations," Tina replied angrily. "This is a complete miscarriage of justice. George Carter has severely beaten his wife and it is his mental state that you should be investigating."

"It does sound as if she has a point," the female police officer said and received a withering look from Jane Price.

"Detective Inspector, it is your job to ensure I receive access to the children. Nothing this woman says is pertinent to the reason we are here. A mentally unstable woman is locked alone in a room with two vulnerable children. I would like to see you take some action to gain access to the children."

"The children are quite safe," Tina said evenly, suppressing her desire to scream at the woman. She had to control her emotions. She needed to use reasoned argument to get them out of her home. "My brother is also in the room. He locked himself in with them as Rose isn't familiar with the workings of the room."

"Then he can open the door," Jane Price stated.

"What's your brother's name?" DI Sharpe asked.

"Peter."

"Peter, I need you to open the door to the room," DI Sharpe said out loud. "I need you all to come out or I will be forced to arrest you and your sister for obstructing justice."

The buzzer announcing someone was at the gate caused everyone to turn in the direction of the sound. Tina walked to the wall, looked at the picture of the gate and pressed the button to admit the man in the car.

"Who is that?" DI Sharpe questioned.

"An old friend," Tina replied.

Tina opened the front door and waited for Jenkins to park the car. They hugged on the doorstep and he followed her back into the house. She just had time to whisper to him that they had visitors.

"This is my friend, Jenkins," Tina announced.

Jenkins went to each person in turn and shook hands. He showed no emotion when he discovered the roles of the visitors.

"This isn't a good time for a social visit," DI Sharpe suggested. "Perhaps you could come back another time?"

"I'm going to be staying here for a few days," Jenkins replied. "I've travelled all the way from South Wales."

"Can we get on with this?" Jane Price demanded. "I don't have all day."

DI Sharpe looked into the camera. "Mrs. Carter, you need to come and speak with me. May I suggest that as a first step you leave the children in the room and come out by yourself. I promise to listen to what you have to say and if your husband has been beating you, then we wouldn't try and remove your children."

"It is not for you to decide," Jane Price said testily. "She may simply have fallen over."

"I have very clear guidelines for these situations," DI Sharpe snapped back. "If Mrs. Carter shows signs of abuse my first priority is to ensure her safety."

"The children's safety is paramount," Jane Price emphasised. "Mrs. Carter has a drinking problem. The children will be safest with their father."

"Who says she has a drinking problem?" Tina challenged. She wondered if the previous night's drinking was actually a regular occurrence, which would explain why Rose hadn't suffered from a hangover.

"She lost her license a few years back for drink, driving," Jane Price replied. "Her husband says she regularly drinks too much."

"Her husband is hardly impartial," Tina exclaimed.

"I'm going to call Powell," Jenkins said.

"Who is Powell?" DI Sharpe enquired.

"A family friend. He was at Mrs. Carter's yesterday when an attempt was made on her life."

DI Sharpe was suddenly lost for words. Even Jane Price seemed surprised by Jenkins' revelation.

"That is the reason she came to stay with me," Tina explained.

"This doesn't ring true," Jane Price stated firmly.

"Two police officers were also attacked," Jenkins explained. "Should be easy for you to check the facts with your colleagues in the Met."

"Were you really not aware of what happened?" Tina asked, trying desperately to hide the hostility she was feeling.

DI Sharpe shifted uncomfortably from one foot to the other. "I wasn't told about any attacks on Mrs. Carter. From her husband or elsewhere." He scowled at Jane Price before continuing, "If Mrs. Carter could come down now and show me her bruises, I think this can quickly be cleared up. Social Services are obviously not in possession of all the facts."

"I am under instruction to take the children back to their father," Jane Price stated but with less conviction than previously.

"I am going to place a call and check up on yesterday's attack," DI Sharpe said to Jane Price.

"You should also speak to Powell," Tina encouraged. "He was at the house at the time of the attack."

Everyone's attention was captured by the sudden appearance of Rose Carter. Tina walked to stand beside Rose and put her arm through Rose's to offer support. The bruises on her face were instantly recognisable.

"Are you Rose Carter?" DI Sharpe asked.

"Yes I am."

"Perhaps you could make us all a cup of tea?" DI Sharpe suggested, looking at Tina and managing a small smile. "I'll join you in a minute."

"Sounds a good idea," Tina agreed.

As everyone followed Tina, DI Sharpe called out, "Jenkins, can I have a quick word, please?"

Jenkins hung back until the others had left and waited for DI Sharpe to speak.

"What do you do for a living?" DI Sharpe asked.

"I suppose you would describe me as an odd job man."

"You look like you could be a bouncer."

"I used to be in the army and like to keep fit but I've never been a bouncer."

"Are you here to protect Mrs. Carter?"

"I really am an old friend of Tina's just paying a visit. I've never met Mrs. Carter before."

DI Sharpe didn't look convinced, "Would you mind calling your friend Powell. I'd like to speak with him about yesterday's events. I will try and speak with someone at the Met but it could take some time to track down the right person."

"Okay," Jenkins agreed. "I'll call him right now."

CHAPTER FOURTEEN

Powell had struggled to fall asleep and awoken several times thinking he heard suspicious noises. The noises were only in his dreams but real enough to make him twice get up and check for intruders. He had finally fallen into a deep sleep just as his alarm rang. He could hear movement in the bathroom but intruders didn't usually take a shower so he dressed and went downstairs to make coffee.

Afina came down at eight and started on the morning routine of preparing the bar for serving breakfast. Powell was pleased there was no further interrogation. He resisted the urge to call Brian, as he knew his friend would call back as soon as he had any information.

When his phone rang, Powell thought Jenkins was just phoning to confirm he had arrived at Tina's. After a brief explanation of events, Jenkins handed the phone to DI Sharpe. Powell recounted the previous day's events. He was relieved the police officer seemed sympathetic and promised he wouldn't be removing Rose's children.

An hour later, Powell received a further call from Jenkins to confirm the police and Social services had left the house, without the children. Understandably, Rose was panicking and immediately started packing. She wanted to run away someplace where they couldn't be found by her husband. She feared the police and Social Services would return. Jenkins had convinced her to stay put at least until he had spoken with Powell.

Powell shared Rose's concern that it was no longer safe for her to stay at Tina's house. George Carter had proved he was a threat to be taken seriously. He had tried to reclaim his children through official channels but his previous actions proved he was not averse to using extreme violence and acting outside the law.

Powell decided he would head straight for Nottingham. Afina didn't want him hanging around the bar so he was killing two proverbial birds with one stone. He spoke to Rose, who promised to remain at the house until he arrived.

He then called Brian and provided an update before asking, "Do you have any news?"

"The bank account used to pay your visitors is an offshore account in the Cayman Islands. The name on the account hasn't yet thrown up anything useful. The phone is registered to a company. Care to guess where it's registered?"

"Cayman Islands?"

"Correct. However, we can at least track where the phone has been recently. That might throw up something more concrete."

"What about Carter?"

"He isn't a person of specific interest to the service. Gets a clean bill of health from the Director, although I didn't say why I was asking. The Director says Carter is a solid establishment figure with many friends in high places. I was warned to stay away and in no circumstances were you to go near him."

"Me!"

"Yes. The Director's no fool. I was fishing for information and in the past when that has happened, you are usually involved somewhere in the background."

"What did you say?"

"Nothing. There was no point in lying. But we need to tread carefully."

"Agreed. Let me know what you find."

Powell found himself looking over his shoulder and checking out his fellow train passengers on the journey to Nottingham. He had a sense of déjà vu as he spotted Tina waiting for him as he exited the barriers. It had only been twenty four hours since they went through the same ritual of hugging and kissing on the cheeks.

Back at the house, Powell asked everyone except the children to assemble in the living room.

"We need to make some decisions," Powell announced. "Two men were waiting for me when I returned home last night..."

"What did they want?" Rose interrupted.

"I think they wanted to extract your whereabouts from me."

"What did you tell them?" Rose asked.

"Nothing. I persuaded them to leave."

"How did you do that?" Rose asked naively.

Jenkins smiled. "Powell has a special knack for getting people to do as he wants. If there were only two of them, they never had much chance. Did you find out anything useful from them?"

"A phone number and bank account details belonging to whoever hired and paid them. I've passed the details to Brian but he says they are both registered in the Cayman Islands so expectations are low. Rose, did your husband have any dealings in the Cayman Islands?"

"Not that I specifically know of but he has business interests all over the world. He's a very wealthy man."

"If you give me the bank account details, I'll see what I can find out," Samurai offered.

"I'll do that but keep your focus on trying to trace the Chairman email account."

"Will do."

Tina was frowning. "I don't understand why these men would have wanted to get Rose's location from you. Her husband knew they were all staying here."

"That has me confused," Powell admitted. "Perhaps they wanted confirmation. I don't know."

"What are you going to do?" Tina asked.

"We've been lucky so far," Powell stated. "That's because they've had to act quickly and have underestimated us. George Carter and his friends are not going to give up. In fact, I expect them to make their next move within twenty four hours. I think we have to assume everyone in the house is in danger. They won't want to leave any possible witnesses."

"We need to move," Rose stated emphatically. "It isn't safe here."

"This house has some advantages," Powell replied. "A big perimeter wall; CCTV; a safe room."

"You think we should stay?" Rose queried doubtfully. "What if the Social Services return to take my children?"

"I don't think that's likely but it is something to consider. My vote would be to hole up here for a few days while Brian and Samurai use technology to try and discover more about who we are fighting. But I'm only one vote. What do you think Tina?"

"I'd rather be here than in some hotel in the middle of nowhere," Tina replied.

"I agree," Samurai concurred. "I'm buried with work."

"Rose?" Powell prompted.

"I'll do whatever you think best."

"Then it's settled. We stay here for the time being at least. We need to take some precautions. Nobody must leave the house unless accompanied by Jenkins or myself. That includes going in the garden and especially applies to the kids. You need to be able to get to the safe room quickly in the event of trouble."

"We could do with some weapons," Jenkins suggested. "Just in case they decide on a frontal assault."

"We will have to innovate," Powell replied. He didn't want to mention in front of the women, the fact he was armed.

CHAPTER FIFTEEN

He travelled on an American passport, which said his name was Brendan Cooley. He landed at Heathrow mid-morning and cursed the long queue at passport control but when it came to his turn, he was quickly admitted, which wouldn't have been the case if they had known his real surname. He had kept the same first name as he would just find it too odd being called anything but Brendan.

He had plied his trade mostly in the States for the last eighteen years. The Good Friday agreement may have led to peace and prosperity in his home country of Ireland but it had put him out of business. It had become unacceptable to kill Catholics. At the time he'd believed the agreement was the thin edge of the wedge. The British intended to allow a united Ireland. It was just a matter of time. He wasn't going to give up his weapons. The IRA could never be trusted.

So he hadn't listened to the politicians and continued doing what he did best. He continued to hunt down and kill members of the IRA. Ignoring the Agreement had quickly seen so called friends melt away. He became a pariah and was betrayed to the security services by his former friends. However, he escaped by the skin of his teeth and found his talents were very much appreciated on the other side of the Atlantic, where his skills were for hire to the highest bidder.

Recently, he had been working almost exclusively for someone who liked to call himself the Chairman. He could call himself whatever he liked, given he had chosen to pay a significant retainer for his services and twice the normal fee for each assignment.

Cooley wasn't altogether happy about his work taking him to the UK. He preferred jobs almost anywhere else in the world, where there was little chance of being recognised by someone with an old score to settle. At least England was safer than Ireland. The risk was minimal but it did exist.

Because of the nature of his work, there was no woman let alone children in Cooley's life. He spent more time in hotels than at the exclusive apartment he rented in New York. He had no attachments, which meant he could disappear at a moment's notice. A necessity in his line of work.

When he wanted the company of women, he paid for his pleasure. A blonde one day and a brunette the next or perhaps both together. He enjoyed his work but even more, he enjoyed the lifestyle it provided. Growing up as a protestant on a rough council estate in Belfast, he could never have dreamed of such a lifestyle.

He was approaching fifty and had begun thinking about when would be a good time to retire. Then he might settle down on some exotic island with a house on the beach. He would spend his days fishing and he might even find himself a girl to share his bed. The idea was becoming more appealing with the passing of each year.

He had received a brief message telling him to head directly to Nottingham, which was a change of plans from his original instructions to go to Brighton. His targets must be on the move. In any event, he had to first go into London to pick up the tools of his trade. He wouldn't be using poison like he had in Singapore.

It took almost six hours from when he exited the airport in his hire car, until he reached the outskirts of Nottingham. A reservation had been organised at a hotel nearby to where his targets were supposed to be staying, situated just off the M1 motorway close to Hucknall. It wasn't an area of the country he had ever visited. He didn't know much of England outside of London. He viewed the close proximity of the motorway as a bonus.

He had an address and simple instructions. Every adult in the house was to be eliminated. As that was five people, it was going to be a very rewarding piece of business. There were also two children in the house but they were not to be harmed. He would have killed them if ordered but was happier they were to be left alive.

There were three male occupants in the house and the instructions came with a warning they should not be underestimated. He never underestimated his targets but the warning was slightly odd. It hinted at more than it said. He wondered if he was following in someone else's footsteps. Had there already been a failed attempt on the targets? He wasn't unduly bothered. His fees were large for good reason. He was the best at what he did and never failed.

He parked his car a discrete distance from the house. It was one in the morning and the road was deserted. He moved closer to the house and crouched in the bushes directly across from the front gate. He pulled the black balaclava over his head and blended into the bushes. He could see frustratingly little beyond the large walls. The house was secluded and the road had no lighting so there was only the moonlight shedding any light on the entrance gate but it was sufficient to spot the camera mounted on the side of the gate.

He was tired and ideally would have waited a day before taking action but his instructions had been clear. Urgency was paramount even if it meant taking a few extra risks but he remained the consummate professional. Although it wasn't strictly necessary, ingrained habits kicked into gear. There were no pedestrians about but he still moved quietly, careful not to step on any dry sticks, which might reveal his presence. His breathing was even and he listened out for any sounds that could be of human or animal origin but nothing disturbed the quiet of the night.

He circled the house as far as the road allowed. A couple of times a car passed and he stayed still until they had disappeared into the distance. When they had gone, the eerie silence once again descended. There was no sign of any further cameras on the walls, which was a little surprising. However, there was glass cemented into the top of the wall to discourage anyone from climbing over. The people inside obviously liked their privacy. His instincts suggested it might be an evening when he truly earned his fees.

No matter the urgency of the job, he needed more equipment than the small amount of explosives in his rucksack and the gun strapped to his shoulder, to gain access to the house. A ladder would be useful but unfortunately they didn't come as standard with hire cars. Neither were there any trees conveniently placed for him to climb over the wall.

It was risky but he had an idea. He returned to the car and drove to the corner of the wall. He mounted the pavement and crossed the strip of grass, reversing the car so it was backing against the wall. He took the rubber mats from the floor of the car and climbed onto the bonnet of the BMW. He then pulled himself on to the roof. He was pleased he had decided to hire an MPV with its greater height.

The top of the wall was now in line with his eyes, which meant it was approximately twelve feet tall. He placed the rubber mats on top of each other, covering the top of the wall. He then carefully pulled himself onto the top of the wall. He perched on top for a second and looked down at the other side. There was grass interspersed with some bushes. He turned himself around and hung from the wall before dropping the last six feet to the ground.

He crouched in the darkness and took in his surroundings. The house was about a hundred metres away at the end of a long drive. He hoped none of the occupants suffered from insomnia. At least there were no lights showing. He was no more than a fleeting shadow as he sprinted across the grass towards the rear of the house.

CHAPTER SIXTEEN

Powell and Jenkins had decided to take shifts keeping watch. Samurai had shown them the impressive security features based in the safe room. Sensors in the bushes identified the intruder's arrival in the grounds. Jenkins was on watch at the time and quickly awoke Powell, who was sleeping on the sofa in the safe room.

"We have visitors," Jenkins announced, shaking Powell's shoulder.

Powell was instantly alert. "What do we know?" He immediately pulled on his shoes. He'd slept in his jeans and tee shirt.

"Not much except something or someone broke a sensor close to the wall."

Samurai had explained the ring of sensors were set at a height where the beam couldn't be broken by small animals like rabbits or cats.

"Let's get everyone inside here as quickly as possible," Powell directed.

Within a couple of minutes everyone was assembled in the safe room.

"What's happening," a concerned Rose asked.

"We have an intruder in the grounds," Powell explained. "You all wait here while I go investigate."

"I'll come with you," Jenkins volunteered.

"No. Look after everyone in here," Powell replied firmly. "If I'm not back in twenty minutes, call the police."

Powell didn't wait around to debate his decision. He hurried to the top of the stairs. Taking his gun from his pocket, he stood and listened but could hear nothing out of place so slowly descended the stairs. The thick carpet helped to muffle the sound of his footsteps.

At the bottom of the stairs, he again listened for the sounds of danger but everything was quiet in the house. He moved to the lounge and carefully crossed to the French doors, which led onto the patio. He'd identified them as a point where professional intruders might try to gain access to the house. He was hidden from outside view by the closed curtains. Once he was certain nobody was in the process of gaining imminent entry through the doors, he eased back the edge of the curtain.

There were no floodlights at the back of the house, only at the front, which were activated when anybody approached the front door. Unfortunately, criminals rarely arrived by the front door. Powell stared out into the darkness, trying to identify danger. There was nothing to be seen.

He decided to move to the kitchen, which also had a door to the rear garden. He moved silently, anxious not to alert the intruder to his presence, should he already have gained access to the house.

A dark shadow crossed Powell's periphery vision as he took a few steps inside the kitchen. He instantly lashed out to the side with a kick, without even turning towards the danger.

The shadow grunted.

Powell followed up as he saw the figure in black try to raise his arm. He crashed into the intruder, driving the breath from his body. The gun in the man's hand clattered noisily to the floor.

Powell tried to take a step back to try and put distance between himself and the attacker. However, the man had hold of Powell's shirt, gripping him tightly. He spun Powell around and threw him back against the wall. Powell's spine and head jolted with the impact of hitting the wall and his own weapon fell to the floor.

Powell was momentarily off balance as the man brought a knee up into his groin. Powell brought his own leg up to block the blow but the assailant was relentless. An elbow connected with the side of Powell's head. He was dazed but as a fist rained blows on his head, he knew if he wanted to live, he had to fight back.

Trying to shake of the dizzy feeling, he aimed a kick at the man's knee. It lacked his usual power but was sufficient for the man to loosen his grip.

Powell tore himself free and taking a step backwards, delivered a kick aimed at the man's chest. The man moved out of range of the kick but just as he was considering a further kick, the man launched himself at Powell. He obviously wanted to fight at close quarters, unlike Powell who would have preferred to keep some distance from his attacker.

The man was strong and Powell crashed to the floor with the man on top. Two punches in quick succession landed on Powell's head. Powell raised his leg and wrapped it around the man's neck and pushed him away.

The man reacted quicker than Powell. He resumed his attack as Powell tried to climb to his feet, throwing repeated punches to Powell's kidneys.

The nerve ends in Powell's muscles were complaining. The impact of the man's blows was having an effect.

Powell tried to deliver a chop to the man's throat but his head was bowed and the blow landed instead on the man's forehead. The man continued to pound at Powell's kidneys. He was doing his utmost to incapacitate Powell and it was working.

Powell's right arm managed to deliver a powerful blow to the man's left shoulder. The result was immediate. The man stopped punching as his arm went numb. Powell planned to repeat the blow but the man once again gripped Powell by his clothes and propelled him backwards across the kitchen until his back crashed into the island work surface.

Still the attacker wouldn't let go of his grip. Powell struck out with both fists aimed at the man's chin but barely connected as the man spun him around and threw him to the floor.

Powell couldn't avoid the man's kick as he lay on the ground but rolled away from its full impact. Fortunately, his brain was just about still working. Somewhere on the kitchen floor were two guns. Powell allowed himself to receive a further kick as he desperately scanned the floor for the weapons. He located one of the guns. It was behind the attacker.

As the attacker went for a further kick, Powell swung his legs and connected with the ankle of the man's standing leg, upending him on the floor.

Powell thought he jumped up quickly but was amazed to see the attacker spring to his feet before Powell had time to take any advantage.

Powell warily circled the man. A couple of kicks dissuaded the man from attacking for a few seconds. Finally, Powell achieved his objective. He was now closest to the gun. But he couldn't risk taking his eyes off the man for a second.

Powell took a few steps backwards as if afraid of a further assault. In reality, he was getting closer to the weapon. He glanced behind to check his whereabouts and at that moment the man saw the gun on the floor and realised Powell's intentions.

The man rushed at Powell, who kicked out and caught the man in the midriff. It felt like kicking stone but had the desired effect of sending the man backwards. In the same instant, Powell threw himself to the floor and slid across the tiles to the gun. He wrapped his fingers around the handle and turned back towards his attacker.

He fired at where the man had been standing but he was gone. Powell heard the sound of the kitchen door banging against the wall. He fired in the general direction of the door just as the man was bolting out of the door. He thought he may have hit the man in his trailing arm but wasn't sure.

Powell climbed to his feet. He was feeling a bit dazed and walked slowly to the kitchen door. He was pleased to see a few drops of blood on the floor. He poked his head outside the door but couldn't see any sign of his attacker. The wound hadn't been serious enough to slow the man down. He had made his escape.

Powell had no intention of rushing out into the darkness and risk being ambushed. He was feeling bruised and battered. In fact, he didn't feel like rushing anywhere. He recognised lady luck had been on his side tonight. Was he slowing down or was everyone else simply getting better? Perhaps age was finally taking its toll on his fighting skills.

He moved to the kitchen sink and ran the cold tap, then put his head under the revitalising water. He let the water run on his neck for a full minute until it helped clear his senses.

Before returning upstairs, he found the second gun on the floor. It would come in extremely useful for Jenkins.

CHAPTER SEVENTEEN

Powell was awoken by Jenkins, who had offered to keep watch for the rest of the night so Powell could get some much needed sleep, after his brutal encounter in the kitchen.

"We have a problem," Jenkins announced.

Powell stirred from his sleep a little slower than usual. Although his mind was willing him to move quickly, his body was not so keen. There was a dull ache running throughout his body, interrupted by occasional sharp pains as he climbed off the sofa. What he really needed was a massage but settled for a few stretches.

"What's happened?" Powell asked, hoping the attacker hadn't returned with a bunch of friends.

"Rose has gone and she's taken the kids."

"What do you mean? Gone where? How?"

"The camera on the gate showed her getting into a taxi an hour ago."

"I don't understand. Why didn't you stop her?"

"There are plenty of internal cameras linked to the safe room but nothing outside except on the front of the gate. Ten minutes ago, Tina went to check the kids were okay and they weren't in their room so she checked on Rose and she was also gone. I did a quick check of the garden, then looked back on the CCTV at the gate. It shows Rose and the children getting into a taxi."

"Were they by themselves?" Powell asked, while pulling on his shoes.

"Yes. Apart from the taxi driver."

"What the hell is she playing at?"

"No idea," Jenkins shrugged.

"Check the house phone and see which taxi company she called."

Powell headed downstairs and found Tina in the kitchen. Images of the previous night's fight flashed through his mind. He once again thought how lucky he'd been to come out of it relatively unscathed.

"Can I get you some pain killers?" Tina asked, unable to keep the look of surprise from her face as she saw his battered face.

Powell wasn't surprised. A look in the bathroom mirror had revealed the bruises had flourished overnight. If they recast Beauty and the Beast, he would have a definite chance of getting the main part. "No thanks. Did Rose say anything to you?"

"Nothing," Tina replied, pouring fresh coffee into a mug and handing it to Powell. "She was very scared last night watching the fight on the camera. As we all were. Perhaps she feels safer on her own."

"You watched everything?"

"Did you forget about the cameras? You can see everything that happens in the house from the safe room. It was dark in the kitchen but that kind of made it worse. At times we weren't sure who was winning."

"Neither was I," Powell smiled wryly.

He had forgotten about the cameras. Rose must have watched him fighting the intruder, wondering what would happen if it had been a different end result. The good news was he could get an image of the intruder from the camera and send it to Brian for identification.

Then he remembered the specks of blood by the door. He walked to the door and was relieved to see Tina hadn't yet cleaned up. "Don't clear up these blood spots. They should be able to give us a DNA sample."

"You told me just in time. I was about to start tidying up in here."

"Any idea at all where Rose might have gone?" Powell quizzed. "Did she ever mention anywhere she would go to hide away from her husband?"

"More than once, I heard her say, she would have to go abroad if she ever left him, but she didn't mention anywhere specific. I don't even think she really meant it."

"I took her bloody phone off her when she came up here so we have no way of contacting her."

"You don't think she could have gone back to her husband?" Tina asked.

"Your guess is as good as mine."

"I only ask because when we were talking the night before, she did mention it might be for the best. I told her not to be so stupid and she didn't mention it again. I don't want to say anything out of turn but she's a bit odd. She drinks too much and admitted he's been hitting her for years. She hinted she left him once before but went back to him. I asked her why and she just shrugged her shoulders. I can't pretend to understand the woman."

It was the first confirmation Powell had received that Rose had been subjected to long term abuse by her husband. Their marriage had layers of complication he couldn't begin to understand. What made a woman stay with a man who regularly left her with black eyes? Was it because of the children? He understood Rose no better than Tina.

His first thought not to get involved in a domestic had probably been the right one. But this was no longer just about an abusive husband. This had become something far more important and complex.

Jenkins entered the kitchen and headed for the coffee pot. "I have the name of the taxi company," he announced. "But they weren't willing to tell me where they took Rose. They wouldn't even admit they had picked up a fare from this address."

Before Powell could answer, his phone rang, revealing a call from an unknown number. "Hello," he answered.

"It's me. Rose."

"Where are you?" Powell asked, concerned.

"I'm sorry about just leaving without saying anything."

"Where are you?" Powell repeated, hiding his irritation.

"The kids needed a break. We're at Alton Towers."

"The theme park?"

"Yes. It will do the children good to have a day out. They can't stay cooped up in that house for ever. Not after what they have been through over the last couple of days."

"So you're all okay?"

"We're fine."

"Why didn't you tell us what you were planning to do?" Powell queried, genuinely not understanding Rose's actions.

"Because you would have tried to talk me out of going."

It was a fair point. Powell knew he would have vetoed the idea. "Where are you calling from?" he asked pleasantly.

"I'm using a payphone at a service station on the M1. We're still about twenty minutes from the park. It doesn't open yet so we stopped for breakfast."

Powell said nothing for a second. He was relieved to hear Rose and the children were safe but still wasn't happy they had just taken off without saying anything. If he was to help her, there had to be mutual trust. Over the phone wasn't the right time to discuss the subject any further. "Your taxi is going to be expensive," he said lightheartedly.

"It's worth it to see the smile on the children's faces."

"I guess you should be safe there. I tell you what. How about Jenkins and I join you at the park in a couple of hours?"

"That would be great. I need someone to go on the scary rides with the children."

"I happen to know Jenkins loves rides," Powell replied, looking across the kitchen to Jenkins. "We can't contact you so let's arrange to meet by the entrance at eleven."

"Thanks, Powell."

"For what?"

"Not shouting at me. Saving our lives. Everything!"

"We'll see you at eleven," Powell confirmed and ended the call. "You and I are off to Alton Towers," Powell announced, looking at Jenkins. "I'll tell you more in the minute but I must call Brian."

Powell began by updating Brian on the previous night's attack.

Brian listened without interruption then commented, "You had a narrow escape."

"I know. He left a few drops of his blood behind. Do you have someone you could send to the house to take a sample and test the DNA? See if we can identify our visitor."

"I'll get right on it. I'll call Tina to let her know when to expect someone."

"Thanks. Let's hope his DNA is on file. But keep this unofficial."

CHAPTER EIGHTEEN

Jenkins drove the hour and ten minutes to Alton Towers. Powell was a quiet passenger as he was lost in his thoughts. He hadn't visited a theme park for over ten years and there was a tinge of sadness as he recalled the last time he had taken his daughter to Thorpe Park. He had intentionally kept busy since Bella died but every so often something would prompt a particular memory. Not that he was trying to forget Bella and he thought of her every day. Indeed, he spoke to her every day and hoped she was somehow listening.

Sometimes his memory was triggered by something quite mundane but this occasion was different. It had been a sunny day much like today and it had been Bella's birthday treat. There was a photo on the wall at home of the two of them getting splashed on the water ride. He had looked at the photo every day for many years.

"This will be good for the kids," Jenkins said, interrupting Powell's thoughts.

"You're right," Powell agreed. "They deserve to have a fun day out."

"I can't imagine what it's like, seeing your father beat up your mother."

Powell thought it would scar children for life. "Rose told me, he never hit her in front of the kids. He would take her to the bedroom."

"Didn't she refuse to go?"

"She would go with him, despite knowing what he would do to her, because she didn't want the children to see her being hit."

"She's a brave lady," Jenkins said. "And he's a right bastard. I'd like to give him a taste of his own medicine."

"You will have to get in line. I'm at the front of the queue."

They sat quietly for a few minutes. Then Jenkins broke the silence. "I'm looking forward to going on The Smiler. It's meant to be a great ride. It's only been open a short time."

"I hate roller coasters. I can't see the attraction. They scare me to death."

"You can't be serious?"

"I'm very serious."

Jenkins laughed. "But I've seen you do really scary things and never hesitate for a second."

"I'm not an adrenalin junkie like you. I just do things because it's necessary. I like to keep my feet on the ground. You won't catch me jumping out of aeroplanes or doing bungee jumps either. I'm always reading about faulty equipment causing accidents."

"Come on Nemesis with me then. It's not very scary."

"I'm not a complete idiot! They don't name a gentle ride, *Nemesis*."

"I bet Rose's kids will want to go on the big rides."

"Then they can keep you company."

"Your secret is safe with me. I promise I won't tell anyone you're scared." Jenkins held his hand up to reveal his fingers were crossed.

"Rides are for kids. Unlike some people I know, I've grown up."

"Talking of kids, it might be best to keep away from them as much as possible. Your face looks quite scary."

"At least I have an excuse for how I currently look."

The banter ceased as they approached the entrance to Alton Towers. The car park was relatively empty due to it being a weekday and not a school holiday. Jenkins parked and they were inside the main entrance by ten minutes to eleven. They had decided to leave their weapons behind as there would be security checks on the entrance and they didn't want to get into a firefight in a park frequented mostly by women and children.

Rose and two very excited children came running over five minutes later.

"I'm sorry," Rose said by way of introduction.

"Don't worry," Powell replied. "I'm not sure whether your children or Jenkins are the most excited about being here."

"Who is up for going on Nemesis?" Jenkins asked.

Both children answered in chorus, "Me."

They headed towards the ride and what turned out to be a relatively short queue as it was a school day.

After a couple of hours of different rides, the children were complaining of being hungry so they all headed towards somewhere selling burgers.

Powell had started to relax and was no longer considering everyone who looked in their direction a potential threat. They found a table outside and Powell went inside with Rose to order the food. The children were happy to remain with their new best friend – Jenkins, who had accompanied them on every ride.

When Powell returned outside to find the table vacant, he scanned the vicinity but there was no sign of Jenkins or the children.

"Where are they?" Rose asked, placing the tray of drinks down on the circular wooden table.

"Probably went to the toilet. I'll go and check."

Powell headed to the nearby toilets but there was no sign of them. He hurried back to Rose.

"What should we do?" a frantic sounding Rose asked. She started calling out their names.

Powell approached a couple sat at a nearby table. "Excuse me. Did you see where the man and two children sat at that table, went?"

The man replied. "I think they went off with the balloon man. They won a VIP pass or something. Is everything all right?"

"Was the balloon man by himself?"

"There were two other men."

"Did you see which way they went?"

"They headed over that way. The one with the Irish accent said something about going to collect their VIP passes."

"They've got my children," Rose shrieked.

"Come with me," Powell instructed and grabbed hold of Rose's hand.

"Where are we going?"

"To find the kids."

"We should tell someone what's happened. Call the police."

"We don't have time."

Powell was pulling on Rose's hand, forcing Rose to walk quicker than she was able. He hurried in the direction the man had pointed. There was a narrow path, which led to the back of an ice cream hut that wasn't open. Powell bent down and picked up a couple of cloths from the ground. He held them to his nose and recognised the smell of chloroform.

"What is it?" Rose asked.

"Chloroform."

"Oh God! What have they done to them?"

"It just puts them to sleep. It means they haven't harmed the children. They probably intend to take them back to their father." Powell was hoping Jenkins was okay. The men who had taken the children might not intend to harm them but Jenkins would be a different matter.

"He mustn't get my children," Rose cried.

"I know it's difficult but you need to try and remain calm. He hasn't got them yet. Come on."

"Run ahead," Rose encouraged. "I'll slow you down."

"I'm not letting you out of my sight," Powell replied firmly.

"Just find my children," Rose begged.

"We'll find them together. Stay close to me."

Powell took hold of Rose's hand and started jogging towards the exit. There was no immediate sign of the children. He was wondering how the men had managed to get the children out of the park without attracting too much attention. There wasn't time to stop and question the staff. He continued towards the car park.

He could hear Rose breathing heavily. She was struggling to keep up the pace even though he was taking it very slowly. She obviously wasn't someone who spent time at the gym.

They arrived at the car park and he desperately scanned the cars but there was no sign of the children. Rose was bent double trying to catch her breath. Tears were pouring down her face.

Powell noticed a man in a suit, who looked out of place. He seemed familiar and Powell realised he was one of the men, who two days earlier had pretended to work for BT. He was making no attempt to disguise the fact he was staring straight at Powell and Rose.

Then Powell saw the van close by the BT man. Another man was pushing a wheelchair into the back before closing the doors and hurrying to the driver's side. So that was how they had taken the children out of the park.

Powell was now more concerned for Rose's safety than the children. He had to assume their father wouldn't want them to come to harm. If anything, they were a bargaining chip. Rose was a different matter. George Carter wanted her dead.

Powell spotted the second BT man. He must have been circling the car park. The result was that the two men were now approaching from each side.

"We need to move," Powell instructed.

He took Rose's arm and pulled her towards the nearest couple just remotely unlocking their car.

"This is an emergency," Powell explained as he took the man by the wrist and removed his keys. The man was skinny and in his twenties. Powell easily pushed him aside.

"What the hell are you doing?" the man demanded, staggering backwards.

Powell opened the passenger door and pushed Rose inside. The young woman stood open mouthed to the side. The husband showed no inclination to try and forcibly stop Powell.

"Help," the man shouted at the top of his voice, "They're stealing my car."

A couple of people looked in the direction of the man but Powell was already starting the car and pulling away. The van had disappeared from sight.

As Powell moved forward towards the exit, both BT men ran

towards the car. Powell wanted to go faster but there were other cars up ahead getting in the way. He pulled out of the line and accelerated down the outside of the queue of traffic. One of the cars close to the exit was slow to move and Powell shot into the space.

The first BT man was closing on the side. He had a weapon in his extended arm.

"Get down," Powell shouted at Rose.

There were no cars entering the park so Powell accelerated again and pulled out into the oncoming lane. He put his foot to the floor and sped past the BT man.

A bullet shattered the glass on the passenger side of the car and Powell was relieved to see Rose had done as instructed and was hugging the floor.

Powell glanced at his rear view mirror and could see BT man running hard away from the exiting traffic, probably back towards his car. Powell swung out onto the main road and received a noisy blast on a horn for pushing into the smallest of gaps in the traffic.

CHAPTER NINETEEN

Powell was staring hard into his rear view mirror. Rose had sat back up and was twisted around in her seat, looking out of the rear window.

"Are we being followed?" Rose queried.

Powell had no doubt the BT men were not going to give up the chase. He identified a car driving fast and overtaking other cars. He wished he'd stolen a faster car than the Ford Focus he was driving. The car behind looked like a BMW and was quickly closing the gap.

"I think there's a silver BMW giving chase," Powell replied.

He suddenly remembered to check the petrol gauge and was happy to see a half full tank.

"I see it!" Rose exclaimed. "What are you going to do?"

"I'm not sure."

"What about my children?"

"Listen, Rose. The children are at least safe. If your husband had wanted them harmed, those men I assume he hired, wouldn't have gone to so much trouble to get them out of the park. You're an entirely different matter. In some ways, the kids are safer well away from you."

"But…"

"Rose, that man back at the park fired a bullet at us. He was trying to kill one or both of us. You are no use to your children, dead. We need to concentrate on getting out of here alive. Then we can worry about the children."

Powell saw the road ahead fork and at the last moment he took the left turn. He needed to get off the main road. The car would have been reported stolen and the local police would be on the lookout. He hadn't seen the van again and it was quite possible it had turned in the opposite direction when it exited the car park. Even if it was further up the road, he wasn't going to be able to run it off the road with the children inside.

He concentrated on getting every last bit of speed from the car. The road was twisting and turning. The car behind wasn't able to use its superior power and wasn't gaining but neither was it dropping any further behind. Powell took one corner too fast and felt the rear slide as he gripped the steering wheel and adjusted.

Rose gave out a small cry of fear.

"Sorry," Powell apologised and tried to smile reassuringly. "I've had advanced driver training."

Rose gripped the handle above the door. "Shouldn't we call the police and tell them my children have been kidnapped?"

"I know you don't want to hear this but I think we have to ignore the children for the time being. Whoever took the children is armed and extremely dangerous. We don't want the children at the centre of a gun battle, which is what might happen if the police get involved."

"But what if you're wrong? What if my children aren't safe?"

"You need to trust me. Right now, it's you they are after silencing."

"But why? I can't testify against my husband."

"No. But you can reveal details of his involvement in a terror attack and maybe more. It's not the sort of publicity he or his friends are willing to risk."

"Let me have your phone," Rose requested.

"Who are you going to call?"

"I'm going to call George."

Powell could see no harm in the idea so passed across his phone. As he did so, he was struck by his own stupidity. He had removed Rose's phone before they left London but his phone was equally as easy to track. Perhaps he and Jenkins had been followed to Alton Towers and caused the children to be taken.

"Put it on speaker," Powell said. "So I can hear."

It seemed the call might go to voicemail but at the last moment was answered.

"George Carter," he answered, slightly uncertain.

"It's Rose."

"I didn't expect to hear from you," Carter said, surprised. "Is this your new phone?"

"No. I just borrowed it to call you. Is the reason you are surprised to hear from me because you thought I'd be dead by now?"

"Don't be so stupid, Rose. Why would I want to harm you?"

"Did you take the children?"

"Am I on speaker phone by any chance?"

"Yes."

"You are the one who took the children, when you ran away with your lover. I suppose that he is listening to our conversation right now."

"George, are the children safe?" Rose screamed into the phone.

"Of course they are safe. I wasn't going to let you and lover boy have my children."

"You know I don't have a lover."

"That's not what I hear."

"Do you swear the children are safe?" Rose repeated.

"They are my children," Carter emphasised. "Why would I hurt them?"

"I'm your wife but it never stopped you hurting me."

"Children and wives are not the same thing."

"You won't get away with this," Rose threatened.

"Get away with what exactly?"

"Someone tried to shoot me ten minutes ago."

There was a pause at the end of the phone. "I don't believe you. You're being delusional. More proof why the children should stay with me."

"Fuck you," Rose swore and ended the call.

"You need to remain strong," Powell said. "We'll get your children back."

"I agree they are safe," Rose replied and sank back into the seat. "I can't believe how someone could change so much. He wasn't a bad man when I married him."

Powell didn't feel inclined to comment. His experience of relationships was decidedly limited. He could see how George was cleverly painting a picture of the unfaithful wife running off with her lover. He was blackening her reputation. Anything she said would be less believable.

Right now, that was the least of Powell's concerns. The car behind was visible in the distance on the occasional straight stretch of road. He needed a better plan than hoping the BMW would be the first to run out of petrol. The road signs said they were heading towards Ashbourne.

"I'm not sure where I'm going, Rose. Can you check on my phone and find out if there is a taxi company in Ashbourne."

Rose picked up the phone and started searching. "There are a couple of firms."

"Now check if there is a supermarket."

"There's a Sainsbury's."

"Can you please put the post code in the Sat Nav."

Rose did as asked. Powell checked to see the estimated time to arrive was showing as twelve minutes.

"Call the taxi company and get them to pick us up in ten minutes from in front of Sainsbury's. Tell them we need to go to East Midlands airport."

Powell listened while Rose phoned and booked the taxi without any problem.

"I don't have my passport with me," Rose pointed out.

"That's okay. We're not flying anywhere. When we get to Sainsbury's we have to move fast."

Powell had Rose help him wipe all evidence of their finger prints from inside the car. There was no need to make it easy for the police.

He accelerated and drove the last few miles even more recklessly. On the edge of town, he was forced to slow but he went through red lights and hoped that would buy him a further minute's advantage.

The Sainsbury's was right in the centre of town. He turned into the entrance confident the pursuers hadn't seen him make the turn. He drove right up to the front of the store and parked in a disabled space.

"Let's go," he shouted to Rose.

There was a taxi waiting just twenty metres away. They ran to the taxi and threw themselves in the back.

"We're running late," Powell explained.

The driver responded by pulling away. "What time is your flight?" he asked.

"We're not flying. We're meeting someone. They were due to land about now so I reckon it will take them about half an hour to clear customs."

As they were about to turn out on to the main road, Powell reached across and put his arm around Rose. He pulled her close so she was leaning into his shoulder. It meant she could barely be seen from outside the taxi. He put his head in his hand so he too would be difficult to identify.

The taxi turned out of Sainsbury's and headed back in the direction from which Powell had driven. He spotted the BMW approaching slowly as it was stuck behind several cars in no hurry. Powell bent towards Rose and pretended to kiss her as they passed the BMW.

He waited until they were well past the BMW before risking a look behind. He was pleased to see the BMW was continuing on its way. He allowed Rose to sit back up straight.

He took his phone from his pocket and called Tina to tell her they wouldn't be returning to the house and he would call her later to explain. Then he turned off the phone. He wasn't sure it was being tracked but it was best not to take the risk.

Powell didn't like the idea of the weapons being left at Tina's house but didn't have a choice. It was possible the house was being watched. Someone could even have followed Rose to Alton Towers. The taxi was now taking them in the opposite direction to where Tina lived. Hopefully there would be no more trouble for Tina and Samurai.

Sitting in the back of the taxi gave Powell the chance to think about Jenkins. Powell desperately hoped he was alive. At least his dead body hadn't been laying on the ground back at Alton Towers. He was of no value to George Carter or his friends. They had no reason to want him dead.

He must have already been in the back of the van by the time Powell arrived at the car park and saw them putting the wheelchair in the van. Or was that wishful thinking? Why would they waste time taking Jenkins with them? Powell had a very uneasy feeling in the pit of his stomach.

CHAPTER TWENTY

The Chairman wasn't used to receiving so much negative news. People rarely failed him once let alone twice. Carter's wife was proving to be unexpectedly elusive. Her husband had foolishly dismissed the possibility of her causing any problem. So much for his claim of having her under control! She was a very loose cannon.

The Chairman hoped he was not backing the wrong horse in selecting Carter to be the next piece in the jigsaw. He was something of a compromise. The best of a bad bunch. The Chairman didn't like the reports he had recently received about the man's personal life. Hitting your wife was bound to eventually lead to the wrong kind of publicity. And anyway, it was just wrong. The Brit would need careful monitoring.

The Chairman was pleased with his decision to book the Irishman on the first plane to England. Brendan was always reliable and Powell was proving extremely problematical. It was wrong not to have properly briefed Brendan about Powell's capabilities but it was no one's fault, as they had thought him to be a run of the mill civilian. It had taken some time and pulling in a number of favours, for the Chairman to get his hands on Powell's records from MI5 and the police. What the Chairman read was fascinating.

It was now apparent, Powell was far from ordinary. He was not a man to take lightly. Brendan needed to quickly rectify the situation and he had the support of two additional good men. It was a pity, because Powell seemed just the type of man that could be useful to the organisation but that was no longer an option. Powell had been unlucky enough to choose the wrong side.

It seemed to be a day of one difficult phone call after another. This time it was the Chairman's turn to pass on information. He dialled the private number for the President, which was known to only a very select group of his inner circle.

"Hello, Mr. President."

"Hello, Ted. That young man in France did well. He's the sort of man we could use on our team."

"I agree. As we don't have anyone French on the team, I'm planning to personally put out some feelers to see if he might be interested in our patronage. I've never met him but with his finance background we have many acquaintances in common."

"I think that would be a very good idea. I had dinner with him and I liked what he had to say. He recognises we have global problems and they need to be tackled by new global partnerships. He is keen on building good relationships with Russia as well as ourselves."

"That all sounds positive, Mr. President."

"But he isn't the reason you called, Ted. What can I do for you?"

"Speaking of Russia, I had a call from our mutual friend in the Kremlin. It seems they aren't very happy. In fact, I've never known them so mad."

"You mean because of what we did in Syria?"

"Yes. They are wondering if your original agreement still holds good?"

"I spoke with Putin and informed him what we did shouldn't be misinterpreted. He's backing the wrong man in Assad. I won't stand by and see women and children gassed. That's a war crime. Anyway, it seems to have done me some good in the polls."

The Chairman had no love of Assad and certainly didn't approve of chemical weapons but more importantly, didn't want to upset the Russians. There could be no solutions to global problems if you isolated the Russians. "I think our friend wants confirmation his plans for the Baltic are still valid. You aren't going to have a sudden change of heart." Getting the President into the White House had involved compromises. Though not a fan of Putin, a deal had been struck that benefited both sides.

"I'll keep to my side of the bargain," The President confirmed. "He needn't worry about that. But tell him I don't want to read about children being slaughtered when they make their move."

"Some collateral damage is unavoidable," The Chairman pointed out.

"True and as long as he doesn't use chemical weapons or anything else banned by the Geneva convention, there won't be a problem."

"Good. I'll relay your confirmation."

"What about that other matter? The one to increase my popularity. Any further thoughts on the timing?"

"There will have to be a bit of a delay. The man I am entrusting with the important part of the plan is out of the country for a short time. We can discuss it again in a couple of weeks."

"Well if we are to go ahead, I don't want to be using anyone but the best. I seem to be doing a little better in the polls this week so it might not be necessary."

The Chairman had to smile. It sounded as if the President might be getting cold feet. The Chairman couldn't blame him for not exactly looking forward to being shot. "Trust me, Mr. President, my idea will make you the most popular man in America."

"I've been giving it a great deal of thought. How about if we change the plan a little? A near miss would have the same impact."

"I'm afraid it wouldn't be as effective. You will be a national hero. I can imagine the speech you will give from your hospital bed, assuring the public that democracy won't be defeated. You will look very statesman like." The Chairman knew the idea appealed to the President's vanity. He just had to conquer his fear of being shot.

"I guess you're right. There certainly should be some good photo opportunities."

"And it will guarantee you a second term in office. You will be able to get some important legislation passed and leave your mark on the country."

There was a brief silence while the President digested the Chairman's words. "Let's do it. Let me know when your man is back. If that's all, Ted. I have a plane to catch. I'm looking forward to a game of golf this weekend."

"That's everything, Mr. President. Enjoy your weekend."

"And you, Ted."

As the Chairman ended the call, he was feeling very pleased with himself. Shooting the President was definitely one of his better ideas. It was fortunate the President hadn't realised that getting shot in the shoulder was going to put an end to his golf playing for some considerable time. Otherwise he might be even more reluctant to go ahead.

CHAPTER TWENTY ONE

Powell led Rose to the arrivals area in the airport and found a car hire desk. He paid for a BMW X3, which was a car he had been recently thinking of buying. It would be a good opportunity to test drive the car for a few days. He wanted something with some power in case he was involved in any future car chases.

Next, he went to Dixons and purchased a pay-as-you-go phone. He decided to turn his normal phone on for a brief period. If it was being traced, then the location of the airport might lead those doing the tracing, to at least consider the possibility they had taken a flight. He called Tina and explained why they wouldn't be returning and reminded her to implement the security improvements he'd advised. Anyone listening would hopefully leave Tina and her brother alone in the future.

Then he called Brian and provided a brief update before requesting, "Can you check whether anyone matching Jenkins' description has been found at or near Alton Towers?" Powell was refusing to listen to the voice in his head, which was telling him Jenkins was going to be found dead in a ditch and it would be his fault.

"I'll get right on it," Brian agreed. "Let's stay positive." He had grown to like and respect Jenkins over the last couple of years.

"Can you also please check whether I've been identified as responsible for stealing the car at Alton Towers?" There were plenty of CCTV cameras in the park but solving car thefts wasn't usually top of the police agendas and matching his photo would involve the use of advanced technology, which wasn't always readily available especially for minor crimes.

"Will do. By the way, I've received the blood sample from Tina's house and sent it for testing. I should know the results in the morning."

"Thanks."

Finally, Powell gave Brian the number of his new phone. Brian knew to only call it from an equally safe number. Powell didn't want to be receiving any calls from numbers associated with his regular contacts, which could lead to his number possibly being discovered and tracked.

Powell had left Rose sitting at the bar while he sorted his new phone and made the calls. When he returned, he found her drinking a large glass of wine. Probably something to steady her nerves but Tina had mentioned, she thought Rose might have a drinking problem. Living with someone who used her as a punch bag, Powell certainly wouldn't blame her for turning to drink. He was going to be driving so ordered a coffee despite the appeal of a large whisky.

"I want to go back to London," Rose said firmly, as soon as Powell was seated. "I should never have left George."

"It isn't safe to go back. Have you forgotten why you left? Those two men who pretended they worked for BT weren't paying you a social visit."

"George probably sent them to scare me. I don't believe George would actually hurt me."

Powell was almost at a loss for words. "Have you looked in the mirror recently? How can you say he wouldn't hurt you?"

"That's different. It was punishment for spying on his computer."

"Punishment! We don't live in the middle ages. There is no excuse for what he did to you."

"I need to see my children. I can't live without them."

"And we'll get them back. I promise. But not your way. George may not want you dead but he isn't in this alone. Someone else is pulling the strings. They may have a very different view to George."

"You really think my life is in danger?"

"This is about more than your children. The man who broke into Tina's wasn't there to recover the children. He was an assassin."

"What do you suggest I do?"

"I think I should take you somewhere safe and out of the way. Then I can concentrate on finding out who is behind all this. I need to identify the Chairman."

"I'm not hiding away somewhere in the middle of nowhere. I want to go back to London so I am close to my children if they need me."

"That's a bit like walking into the lion's den."

"You can take me or I'll make my own way back to London. I'll stay in a hotel. I won't go back to George for the time being but I need to be close to Simon and Imogen."

Powell didn't feel it was right to point out she was being naïve. Rose wasn't thinking straight, which wasn't surprising in the circumstances. Her emotions were in tatters. "How about a compromise? Come with me to Brighton. It's only an hour on the train from London. We need a plan to get your children back. Something that works for the long term and ensures you are all safe. Snatching them back isn't a great solution but I will do it if necessary. The problem is where would you then live? You can't spend every day worried about your husband tracking you down."

Rose thought about the idea for a few seconds. "Okay. I'll come to Brighton with you. At least for the time being."

Powell was relieved Rose had seen sense. "Let's get going. In the car you can tell me everything you know about your husband. I want to know every detail. What he likes to eat? What are his hobbies? Everything."

On the drive to Brighton, Powell kept within the speed limit, despite the temptation to give the new car a chance to show its power. He didn't want to risk attracting the attention of the police. The hire car wouldn't raise any alarms on the number plate recognition systems on the motorway so there was no point in attracting trouble.

If the police had the inclination, they would be able to trace the use of his credit card to the car hire company but that would take time and the type of resources normally only allocated to tracking down a terrorist or serious criminal. He didn't believe he had done anything to deserve such attention. Car thefts were two a penny.

Powell decided as a temporary solution that he would take Rose to a hotel in Brighton, rather than stay at his home, which had already proved to be unsafe. The bar was out of the question. He had promised Afina not to bring down trouble on the bar and put Adriana in danger.

He didn't want to stick Rose in a Travelodge where she might quickly become frustrated. He had decided on the Stanmer House Hotel, on the edge of Brighton; an eighteenth century manor house set in acres of woodland and parkland. In the past, it had been a favourite haunt of Powell's to go for a walk with Bella, especially on a Sunday morning, when they would follow their walk with a long lunch in the stylish restaurant.

Rose was used to a certain lifestyle and the hotel was suitably upmarket. It offered everything she needed for a few days. The open spaces of the park would also ensure she wouldn't feel trapped like a prisoner.

Two hours into the journey, Powell received his first call on the new phone. Not surprisingly it was from the only person who had the number.

"Hi Brian. What did you find out?" Powell asked, feeling nervous about the answer he was going to get.

"Good news. Jenkins was discovered unconscious in some ice cream hut. He's been taken to City General Hospital in Stoke. He has a nasty lump on the back of his head and possible concussion but he'll be okay. They are going to keep him in overnight."

Powell felt a huge sense of relief. "Thank God! Let him know I'm on my way back to Brighton and I'll call him this evening."

"Will do. And you will be happy to learn you are not being hunted by the police. They have the car back and it's well down the list of their priorities."

"Some good news for a change. Any more luck with tracing those bank accounts?"

"Nothing. Just dead ends. That's interesting in itself. Someone has gone to a great deal of trouble to keep their identity secret. Normally, when we find such a pattern, we suspect organised crime."

"I don't think we're dealing with your run of the mill criminals. This is about someone with a terrorist or political agenda."

"I agree but I'm afraid I can't justify the use of further resources to keep investigating. Not without something more concrete to go on."

"Let's hope Samurai finds out something."

"I'll second that. Speak soon."

Powell ended the call with a broad smile. Jenkins was alive and reasonably well. Probably giving the nurses hell.

CHAPTER TWENTY TWO

Powell and Rose ate dinner in the hotel restaurant. The atmosphere between them was strained. Rose was despondent and only picked at her food. She said very little and was obviously exhausted. Powell's attempts to assure Rose the children would be safe with their father, were falling on deaf ears. She was terrified for their safety. He tried to make conversation but was receiving very little response.

Powell was actually in a rather better mood, having spoken to Jenkins, who was sounding in generally good spirits, despite his sore head. Jenkins had been apologetic for allowing the children to be taken and was determined to help get them back. He also fully intended to repay the men for the blow on the head. Powell pointed out the three men who took the children were all armed and so no blame was attached to Jenkins. Powell was grateful Jenkins was alive to fight another day. Powell brought Jenkins up-to-date with events and suggested they talk again in the morning.

It was just after nine when Rose went up to bed. Powell stayed in the lounge to have a nightcap. He needed to unwind further. He also did his best thinking with a whisky in his hand. Over the years he had become used to existing on no more than six hours of sleep. It was partly the result of owning a bar. If he went to bed at ten, he would be awake at four and unable to go back to sleep so he rarely went to bed before midnight.

He needed to call Samurai but couldn't risk using the hotel phones or his mobiles, which could end up being traced back to the hotel. He could think of only one solution. He ordered a taxi from reception and asked to be taken to his bar, which was a fifteen minute journey. He thought it perfectly safe to leave Rose in her room. He didn't expect to be gone long.

It being a Friday night, Powell was pleased to see the bar was busy. Since Afina took over the day to day management, he rarely spent a whole evening at the bar, whereas previously he would spend every weekend working. It was partly that he didn't want to get in her way but also that it was difficult to spend time at the bar without thinking of Bella all the time. It was named after her and memories were ingrained in every inch of the bar.

He smiled at staff as he entered and nodded at Afina to join him, as he went and stood at the end of the long bar counter.

"So you are back," Afina stated.

"Only for a few minutes. I need a favour but first I think I'll have a large Scotch."

Powell could see the bar staff were busy so decided to fix his own drink and walked around the bar.

One of the staff stopped what he was doing and hurried to intercept Powell. "Excuse me, Sir. You can't come behind here."

Afina smiled broadly. "Gus. This is Powell." Seeing no recognition she added, "He owns the bar."

"I'm so sorry," Gus apologised in an Australian accent.

"That's okay, Gus. You weren't to know," Powell replied. "Afina is the important one around here. Not me." Although he was joking, he knew it also to be true.

Powell took his drink and beckoned for Afina to follow him into the office.

"I'm going to use the phone to make a call to Samurai."

Afina looked confused. "You don't need my permission," she joked.

"If anyone should ever ask you about this call, I want you to say you made it. You were trying to find out when I would be returning to work."

"In other words you don't want anyone to know you are back in Brighton?"

"Exactly."

"No problem."

"Is everything okay with you?" Powell asked. "The place looks busy tonight."

"Everything is running smoothly."

"I wouldn't expect anything else."

"The staff are very well trained," Afina emphasised with a smile.

"I know. I'm sorry I leave everything to you to manage."

"I like it that way."

"You mean, when I don't interfere?"

Afina just smiled as an answer. "I should be getting back."

"Listen, would you like to get a drink after you finish? If you don't have plans? I need to unwind a bit."

"You forget. It's Friday. We are open until 1.00am."

"Sorry. It was a stupid idea."

"No it wasn't. It was a good idea but not the best timing."

"Some other time."

"That would be nice. You look tired and your face is bruised. Have you been in a fight?"

"Nothing serious."

"I wonder if the other man would agree with you?"

Powell forced a smiled. "Don't let me keep you."

Afina hesitated for a moment. "Look, give me half an hour and then I can be free. We've taken last orders on food. Adrian can look after everything for a couple of hours. But I have to be back for 1.00am to close up."

"Brilliant! I promise to get you back before you turn into a pumpkin."

"That doesn't make sense. It was Cinderella's carriage that turned into the pumpkin. Not her."

"Yes but it's just a saying. It means I will get you back on time."

"I still don't understand why you would say it but I have learned the English language is specifically designed to confuse foreigners. Now I will leave you to make your call. I will come and collect you when I'm ready."

"Thanks."

Powell was pleased Afina had decided to go for a drink. She was so diligent about her work, he reckoned if she was willing to take time away from the bar on a busy night, it must mean the bruises on his face looked worse than he realised.

He called Tina and they spoke briefly before she then passed the phone to her brother.

"I don't have much news, Powell," Samurai immediately apologised. "I'm afraid I haven't yet been able to discover any identities behind the bank accounts."

Powell hid his disappointment. "That's all right. It was a long shot anyway."

"I did contact a few people to ask if they had come across the email account for the Chairman. I met a brick wall except for one person, who messaged me back and warned me off asking further questions. He is a key player for Anonymous. You know who they are?"

"That group of hackers who wear the funny masks."

"That's them. The person in question is a political activist. We have worked together a couple of times in the past. If he's involved, it's likely something significant is being planned."

"Can we meet this guy?"

"No chance. We chat in forums and know each other by reputation but we would never reveal our true identities. In my line of work, revealing your identity can lead to very unpleasant consequences. He was doing me a huge favour by warning me to stop asking questions."

"Okay. Keep poking around. See what you can find out."

"It won't be easy."

"Just do your best."

Powell ended the call feeling a bit deflated. He had always believed Samurai was capable of hacking any computer and it didn't seem to be the case on this occasion. He was going to have to find answers with more old fashioned methods. That in itself wasn't something he minded doing, except it would inevitably take longer. Samurai's methods were far quicker, when they worked.

Twenty minutes after the call, Afina reappeared in the office.

Powell was surprised to see she had changed into a dress and was wearing makeup.

"You look very glamorous," Powell remarked. "I'm feeling a bit underdressed." He was wearing crumpled jeans and a casual jacket.

"Don't you like my dress?"

"You look beautiful." Although Powell would have said as much if it wasn't true, he hadn't been lying or even exaggerating.

Afina smiled. "Good. Where shall we go?"

"Is Valentino's okay?"

"Perfect. I love their cocktails."

CHAPTER TWENTY THREE

Valentino's had been Powell's favourite cocktail bar in Brighton for many years. It was not somewhere you stumble on by accident if you are new to Brighton or just visiting for the weekend. It is somewhere for locals and the secret of its presence is only shared between good friends. Powell had known the owner for a long time, although he was rarely to be found working in the bar.

Valentino's is a tiny single room, the size of an average living room, in the centre of town, up an unassuming flight of stairs next to the theatre. Powell appreciated the small and intimate atmosphere. It had a very long list of cocktails and was not the type of place that attracted the many hen and stag party visitors to Brighton. It was a civilized bar for grownups. In Summer, Powell liked to sit outside on the tiny balcony where people smoked. He would watch the eclectic mix of people passing on the street below.

Afina wanted to try something different to drink and he had suggested a number of cocktails she might enjoy. He had warned her to stay away from the Shaking Stevens, which he knew was so called because come the morning you would awake with the shakes. In the end, Afina ordered a Mojito and Powell his normal Margherita. He wasn't one for anything sweet or fruity tasting.

"I can't remember the last time just the two of us went out for a drink," Powell said as they sat down with their drinks.

"We've never been out by ourselves."

"That can't be true."

"You've never invited just me out for a drink. We always have Mara, Jenkins or someone with us."

Powell thought about what Afina had said and realised it was true. "I'm sorry. I haven't been avoiding you."

"No need to say sorry. I understand you are afraid of your feelings when you are around me."

"No I am not."

"You are afraid that you will fall in love with me. You are afraid you will end up hurting me. You are afraid I love you for the wrong reasons." Afina smiled broadly. "It's funny. When I met you I didn't think you were afraid of anything."

"I came here for a drink and to relax, not to be psychoanalysed."

"As you wish. But I thought we could be honest with each other."

"English people are not usually so direct."

"Then it is a good thing I am not English. I don't understand why English people never say what they are truly thinking."

"How do you mean?"

"They are always saying sorry even when they don't mean it."

"That's because we are polite."

"And why do people always ask, *how are you,* when they don't really want to know?"

"I think we should go somewhere where they play loud music."

"Why?" Afina asked, surprised by the suggestion.

"Then I can just pretend I can't hear you."

"That is not very polite. Why can't we have a serious conversation for once?"

"Okay. What do you mean by, I'm afraid you love me for the wrong reasons?"

"You have always been worried that I love you because you saved my life. That my emotions aren't to be trusted because of the way we met."

"There is some truth in that," Powell admitted. "You were young and vulnerable. I thought you saw me as the father figure you never had."

"Maybe at first I loved you partly because you were the gallant Englishman who rode to my rescue. You risked your life to save me and my family. But that was a long time ago now. I am no longer vulnerable or immature. I am a woman able to make choices about my life."

"A beautiful, young woman. Whereas I am very close to my sell by date."

"Rubbish. You are in better shape than most boys my age."

"Thank you. But it would never last. You would want children and I can't imagine ever having another child."

"I don't know if I want children but you are probably right, one day I might want a baby with someone I love. I think you are afraid that having another child would somehow be betraying Bella."

Powell said nothing. Bella had been such a special part of his life for so long, he doubted he could ever love another child as much as he had loved Bella and that would be wrong. "Everyone I have truly loved has ended up murdered."

"And if you give your love to me there is always that possibility. We have both come close to death more than once. But do you want in twenty years to look back and regret you never tried to love me?"

Powell was a little lost for words. "I love you already."

"I know but I want to be loved like a woman not a daughter."

"I'm not sure I can."

"With some men I would think it was because of my past. I was a whore. It was not my choice to be a whore but I would understand a man who said that was the reason, he could never sleep with me. But you are not that type of man."

Powell finished his drink. "Would you like another?"

"Yes please. And when you come back we will say no more on this subject. I have said what I wanted."

Powell went to the bar and ordered two more drinks. He looked over his shoulder at Afina, who smiled in his direction. She had changed so much in the last couple of years. She was a successful manager of his business and he had to recognise there was nothing remotely vulnerable about her anymore. She was a confident, young woman, who knew what she wanted from life. Rather bizarrely, she seemed the more mature of the two of them in some ways, despite there being more than a quarter of a century age gap.

Powell was also aware Afina attracted glances from men wherever she went. If he didn't take this chance, it was only a matter of time before someone else would.

He ordered an extra whisky from the barman and downed it in one. The evening was not turning out the way he had planned. Not that there had really been any plan. He had just wanted a drink and some good company.

He returned to Afina with the cocktails. This time, he sat next to her on the leather seat rather than opposite, where he had been sitting before. He reached out with his hand and covered Afina's hand.

"You could do much better than me," Powell said.

"Probably true," Afina agreed light heartedly.

"We must take it slowly."

"You've been taking it slowly for three years."

"Are you sure?" Powell asked.

Afina leaned close and said, "I've been sure for years." Then she kissed him gently on the lips.

CHAPTER TWENTY FOUR

Powell had gone back to the bar with Afina and helped her lock up for the evening. Then they had gone to bed and made love. It was the first time they had ever made love. The sex they had shared when Afina was working for the Romanian pimps, had been an exchange of a service for money. It had been enjoyable sex at the time, at least on his part, but this was something completely different. Afina had made love to him of her own free will and he had not been embarked on a mission to find his daughter's killer.

He had focused on her pleasure and loved it when she climaxed. He had wondered how her terrible past might have affected her desire and responses but he needn't have worried. Afina was as special a lover as he had anticipated. He realised, he was very fortunate she had waited so long for him to come to his senses. She could easily have been stolen from under his nose by someone else. He must have sorely tested her patience.

When they finally made the decision to get some sleep, he had wanted to stay with Afina rather than return to the hotel. He didn't want what they had shared to seem like a one night stand. He remembered to set an alarm, to ensure he could be back at the hotel before Rose was awake.

Waking up beside Afina had been a little surreal. He immediately reached out and touched her, to ensure it wasn't all an alcohol induced dream. Finding her soft, warm skin, he gently pulled her closer. She stirred and soon they were devouring each other's body with even greater urgency than the previous night.

They showered together but their love making had left no time for anything other than a fleeting kiss goodbye before he took a taxi back to the hotel. He had arranged to meet Rose for breakfast at seven thirty. He went to his room and changed his clothes before heading downstairs in urgent need of coffee. He realised he had a permanent grin on his face and was almost skipping into breakfast. He asked the waiter to bring a latte rather than drink the filter coffee, which looked as if it had been standing too long on the hot plate.

Sipping at his coffee, he tried to understand the seismic change in his life that had taken place in one night. Perhaps seeing Rose's relationship with her children had subconsciously reminded him of what he was missing in his life. Not specifically children but simply a deep and loving relationship. He had previously experienced the love of a child and another woman in his lifetime. He didn't want to live another thirty years without ever experiencing similar again. Life's challenges were better shared.

Powell was now faced with a new challenge. He wanted to send Alma a text. She would be busy organising the serving of breakfast in the bar but he wanted to ask if he could see her again this evening? It was Saturday, which was the busiest night of the week in the bar. She couldn't take the night off work so it would have to be another late liaison. Was it appropriate to suggest he saw her again once she finished work? In effect, because of the late hour, he was asking if she wanted to sleep with him again. Damn it, he was too old to play games or try to play it cool. He sent a text asking what time she could be free tonight?

Having finished with the self-analysis, Powell realised Rose was late for breakfast. Given what she had experienced recently, he wasn't entirely surprised. He decided to help himself to the buffet while he was waiting. He returned to his seat with a full English breakfast, feeling hungrier than normal for so early in the day. He smiled at the thought it was probably because of the previous night's exertions.

He finished his breakfast and glanced again at his watch. Rose was now forty five minutes late. Perhaps she had simply decided she didn't want breakfast or maybe even ordered it in her room. Powell had a final cup of coffee and signed for the bill.

His phone announced the arrival of a text message. He was slightly nervous as he checked Afina's response. She suggested he come to the bar about ten. If he came in the rear entrance, he could go straight upstairs to her living room without being seen. He replied in the affirmative and headed upstairs to find Rose, feeling decidedly happy.

As he approached Rose's room, he was a bit surprised to see the trolley parked outside. The door to the room was open so he stepped inside. The maid was changing the bed.

"Have you seen Rose Carter?" Powell asked.

"Who?" the maid asked.

"This was her room," Powell explained.

"I believe she's checked out, sir."

Powell was overcome with a terrible feeling of foreboding. Perhaps she had misunderstood and thought they were only staying the one night. He hurried downstairs to reception. There was no sign of Rose.

"Can I help?" the young girl behind the desk asked.

"Has Rose Carter in room twenty seven checked out yet?"

"Yes, sir. I called a taxi for her early this morning. I think about six."

Where the hell had she gone? He suspected he knew the answer but hoped he was wrong.

"Are you Mr. Powell?" the receptionist asked.

"Yes."

"She left something for you." The girl turned to the boxes on the wall behind the desk and took a letter from the box for room eighteen, where he was staying.

Powell took the letter and walked away from the desk. He tore open the envelope. Inside was a single sheet of paper.

Dear Powell,

I called my husband this morning and asked if I could come home. I know I will never see my children again if I don't go back and a life without my children is something I can't contemplate.

I thank you for all your help and know you will disagree with my actions but George has promised if I return we can all go back to normal life. He needs me back to look after the children and I have promised to be a good wife and support him in his career.

Please do nothing further to interfere in our lives.

Best regards

Rose.

Powell reread the letter barely able to believe its contents. His good mood had been swept away in a second. How could she be so foolish? He had no way of contacting her as he was responsible for taking away her mobile phone.

He stood holding the letter in his hand and swore out loud. The receptionist gave him a disapproving look. There were too many unanswered questions. He couldn't just walk away. Even if he could accept Rose's personal circumstances dictated her going back to her husband, he had seen evidence George Carter was somehow involved with terrorism. He may not have been the instigator. Almost certainly he wasn't but he knew who was responsible. This was no longer just about Rose and her children.

CHAPTER TWENTY FIVE

The only small positive to come out of Rose's disappearing act was Powell could immediately move back home. However, from the hotel he went first to the bar.

"I didn't expect to see you so soon," Afina smiled as Powell found her in the kitchen.

"Change of plans."

"A good change?"

"Not exactly. I'll tell you about it later."

"Shall we go upstairs?" Afina asked. "I can take a ten minute break."

"You mean…?"

"Sorry, I forgot. At your age you probably need more time to recover."

"Not funny! And not true either." He had felt the stirrings of desire the moment he walked into the bar. The thought of making love again to Afina was all consuming.

Afina smiled broadly. "In that case, let's go. We must be quick though; otherwise my boss may accuse me of not doing my job properly."

"I can do quick. If that's what you want?"

"Hmm. Not too quick."

Afina led the way upstairs and within seconds of entering the bedroom, they were frantically pulling at each other's clothes to get naked.

Afterwards, Powell gave Afina a concise version of recent events.

"This Rose needs help," Afina said.

"I'm not sure I should interfere."

"If you hadn't interfered for me, I would still be getting beaten and abused. You saved my life. Rose needs your help. She must leave her husband."

"I agree but I also understand her predicament. She is worried if she leaves him that he will keep the children."

"Surely that isn't legal?"

"Her husband is a Member of Parliament with a great deal of influence. I understand why she is concerned."

"I would like to meet Rose. I will tell her how you helped me. Then she can believe it is possible to escape her husband."

Powell loved that Afina was always willing to help anyone who needed help. She hid the scars of her own terrible ordeal being trafficked but they had to exist. Her strength of character and resilience was amazing.

"We mustn't rush into anything," Powell cautioned.

"But I need to get back to work."

"What do you mean?"

"If you want more sex, you are going to have to hurry."

Rose walked back into her house with her head hung low. She could barely bring herself to look her husband in the eye. He said little but the children were very excited by her return and ran into her arms. Their reaction convinced her, she had made the right decision by returning home.

They demanded she make pancakes, which was something she normally did at the weekend. George was useless in a kitchen and they would be living off fast food if she hadn't returned home. He left them alone in the kitchen to enjoy their pancakes and for a short time, life seemed back to normal.

After about an hour, George reappeared from his office. The novelty of their mum returning, having worn off, the children went upstairs to their computers. George sat himself at the kitchen table and asked Rose to recount the events of the last couple of days. She poured them both some coffee and did as he asked, telling just one lie. She said she had been staying at the Holiday Inn in Brighton. She didn't want her husband knowing where Powell was really staying, in case he tried to take some form of revenge. George listened and said little.

"This better not be some form of trick hatched up by you and Powell to get the children back," Carter warned. "I won't stand for any more of your games."

"I promise it isn't. I'm genuinely sorry for the trouble I've caused. I've made a dreadful mistake. I never wanted to leave you or the children." Rose's voice was pleading. "When the two men came to the house I was scared."

I don't know anything about that," George stated firmly. "I hope you don't think I sent them? I wouldn't cause trouble in my own home."

That sounded plausible to Rose. Perhaps she had made a terrible mistake believing George was responsible. "I was confused. Please forgive me."

"There will have to be a few changes around here. I don't want you seeing that Angela woman again. She's been a bad influence."

Rose acknowledged her agreement with a nod. She had expected him to be in a mad rage the minute she entered the house. The normal pattern would be that he would then start to hit her while blaming her for making him so angry. The violence would always be followed by him climbing on top of her, which was almost worse. It had been a long time since sex was something to be mutually enjoyed.

George seemed different this time. More in control of his temper. Perhaps she had miscalculated how he would react. She regretted ever telling Angela about the speech. If only she hadn't been snooping on her husband's computer. That wasn't the behaviour of a good wife. She had brought all her troubles on herself.

"We'll discuss this further upstairs," Carter instructed.

Rose's heart sank. She knew what going upstairs meant. She thought about refusing but knew that would only make things worse. She had learned in the early days of his violence that fighting back was not an option. She silently followed him up the stairs. Their bedroom occupied the whole of the third floor.

"You must be punished for all the trouble you've caused," Carter said as he closed the bedroom door. "Don't you agree?" He walked to the bedside table and turned on the radio they kept by the bed. He changed it from the news channel to a music channel and turned the volume up quite high. Rose was pleased the children would be unable to hear her cry out.

She found the cold tone of her husband's voice and the apparent lack of emotion scarier than his usual rage. She said nothing. She knew there was no right answer to his question. She wasn't going to give her permission for whatever he was about to do.

"I don't want the children to see you looking a mess," Carter continued. I won't ever hit you again in the face. He started to undo the belt from his trousers. "Remove your clothes and get on all fours on the bed. I'm going to teach you a lesson you won't forget in a long while."

Rose had been under no illusions what returning home meant. It was a price worth paying to be reunited with her children.

After making love to Afina, Powell spent most of the rest of the day planning and preparing. In an ideal world, it would be possible to bring charges against George Carter for his involvement in terrorism and then Rose and her children would be free to get on with their lives. Unfortunately, it was necessary to be more pragmatic. With a wife unable to testify against her husband, the only evidence was a photo of the speech on Powell's phone, which would be easily discredited by a half decent lawyer. Powell would have liked to see George Carter prosecuted but he was more concerned with securing the safety of Rose and her children.

Powell came up with a plan, based on an operation he and Brian had run in Northern Ireland many years before. Powell spoke with Samurai and redirected his hacking skills in a new direction. A direction Samurai was confident he would be able to help. A quick call to Jenkins ascertained he was already on his way to Brighton and keen to find those responsible for his sore head.

Then Powell called Brian and asked for his help with the most important part of the plan.

"It's going to be a lot harder to pull off than that time in Ireland," Brian said.

"I know. Do you have a better idea?"

"If we can convince the right people Carter is mixed up in terrorism, then it could solve Rose's problem."

"But we already agreed we don't have the evidence for a prosecution."

"Even if we did, Carter would never end up in Court. A Member of Parliament involved in acts of terror. Can you imagine the outcry and scandal?"

"So what are you saying?" Powell probed.

"If we can convince the Director of his guilt, he will disappear for a while. After a time, when he's provided every last bit of useful information, his body will turn up on a beach. A friendly Coroner will pass a verdict of suicide. Or some similar scenario."

"I didn't think such actions were still sanctioned."

"Only in very special cases. In the national interest. I believe this would definitely qualify but it would have to be approved by the Prime Minister."

Powell thought about the suggestion for a moment. "I still think we would need more evidence to convince the Director to act. And what if he chose not to act? We would be in a very difficult position, having shown our hand. Meanwhile Rose is in danger. I think we need to try my plan."

"It's your call. At least for the time being. Why don't I update the Director and see if we can get support for your idea. It would make it a lot easier to execute. We can then park the issue of what happens to Carter, at least for the time being."

"Do you think the Director would agree to help?"

"Yes. In fact, I already sounded him out and received a positive response."

Powell realised he sometimes made life difficult for Brian, who always wanted to help but still had to maintain his relationship with his boss at MI5. "We need to work out the details but that sounds good to me."

"Okay. I'll put the wheels in motion."

"Carter and his friends have a great deal of influence. The number of people in the loop must be minimal."

"We know what we're doing," Brian replied, slightly impatiently. "Some people even think we're quite good at this sort of thing."

"Sorry," Powell apologised. "Of course you know what you are doing."

"On a positive note, we've been able to identify the man who attacked you. The DNA belongs to a former Loyalist paramilitary terrorist, Brendan Callaghan. He was a leading member of the UVF. A nasty piece of work credited with killing many Catholics. Last known whereabouts, although it was only an unconfirmed rumour, he'd fled to the States."

Powell had spent time in Northern Ireland in his early days in MI5. He'd had unofficial contact with the UVF. They occasionally shared information on the IRA, who were perceived as the greater enemy. Powell's wife had been killed by IRA terrorists and he had left the Security Services as a result. He had tried to consign Ireland to a part of his mind he rarely accessed. Anything dredging up those memories inevitably made him feel nauseous. The thought, the man he had fought with was Irish made him doubly sick.

CHAPTER TWENTY SIX

It was late in the afternoon when Powell decided it was time to call George Carter. He had obtained his mobile number from Brian.

"George Carter," an uncertain voice answered, which wasn't surprising given Powell had blocked his own number.

"This is Powell."

There were a couple of seconds silence at the end of the phone. Powell wondered if Carter was thinking of simply ending the call.

Eventually Carter's curiosity overcame his suspicions. "What can I do for you, Powell?"

"I was hoping we could meet. I'm suffering some financial challenges and I thought you might be able to help me out."

"Why would I do that?"

"The British climate doesn't really agree with me. I was thinking of living somewhere in the sun."

"I still don't understand what that has to do with me?"

"If I go away, your problems go away."

"I'm not aware I have any problems. At least none that concern you."

"I have a photo of a speech you were due to give. It doesn't add up to much evidence in a court of law but I'm sure I can find an interested newspaper. I think they would pay good money for such a story. If not, I have friends who can ensure the photo appears all over the internet."

"Are you trying to blackmail me?"

"No. I'm a business man. You can't blame me for wanting to make some money. I've had a load of expenses over the last few days. I'm proposing a solution to a problem that works for all of us. It's not really something we can discuss over the phone so we should meet.

What have you got to lose?"

"When and where are you proposing we meet?"

"Do you know the RAC club in Pall Mall?"

"I've been there a couple of times."

"How about we meet at eleven tomorrow morning?"

"You have to be a member."

"I am. I'll be in the Drawing room." Powell didn't need to add he had only been a member since his call to Brian, who would use his contacts to make the arrangements.

Powell had been to the club a couple of times with Brian. It was a bit stuffy for Powell's taste but it was quite close to Victoria and he believed the upmarket location would make Carter relaxed about meeting.

"I'll be there," Carter confirmed and ended the call.

Let the chess game begin, Powell thought as he put down his phone.

Afina gave Jenkins a welcoming hug and gently ran her fingers over the large bump on his head.

"That must have hurt," Afina stated.

"I've always had a hard head," Jenkins joked. "Just as well, since I started working with Powell."

Powell and Jenkins were sat at a table in a corner of the bar drinking beer. Powell had brought Jenkins up-to-date with events and his plan, before Afina came over to say hello.

"Are you hungry?" Afina asked.

"Starving. That hospital served nothing edible."

"Let me guess. A large rib eye with all the extras?"

"That would be perfect."

"Same for me," Powell requested.

"Good idea. You need to keep your strength up."

Afina walked away and Jenkins asked, "What did she mean by that?"

"Don't know," Powell lied. He was in no hurry to tell Jenkins about the change in his relationship with Afina. Jenkins had always been convinced they would end up together and didn't understand why Powell was so slow to act. No need to tell him he was right all along.

"I like your idea," Jenkins said. "The problem is you can't trust Carter to pay you the money. He may not even turn up to tomorrow's meeting."

"I think he'll meet me. He really has nothing to lose. I don't believe he feels threatened by me."

"He may tell his friends about your meeting. You might find them turning up as well."

"If they do, then the trouble will probably come when I leave the club. That's where I need your help."

"I hope they do turn up. I owe them for my headache."

"Well we don't have long to wait and find out."

"On the positive side, I guess that means we can enjoy tonight," Jenkins said. "A couple of beers wouldn't go amiss."

"We should probably take it easy. Tomorrow could be lively."

"I agree. We'll just have a few drinks."

"I really am getting an early night," Powell stressed.

Afina arrived with the steaks. "Two medium rare rib eyes," she announced, placing the plates on the table.

"How's Mara?" Jenkins asked.

"She's well. Perhaps we will get a chance to all go out for a drink."

"That would be great," Jenkins agreed.

"Enjoy," Afina said as she walked away, humming a tune.

"Afina seems in a particularly good mood." Jenkins commented.

"I hadn't noticed," Powell lied.

"That's your problem. You don't realise what you're missing with Afina."

"Like you're the expert on women. You're just as bad with Mara."

"You know it's not the same. Mara is an escort and bisexual. It's complicated."

"Afina and I aren't exactly straightforward. And anyway, you're tri-sexual."

"What the fuck does that mean?"

"You'll try anything."

"Very funny. At least you know Afina fancies the hell out of you if you ever do get off your arse and show an interest. I haven't a clue what Mara thinks of me."

"There's only one way to find out."

CHAPTER TWENTY SEVEN

Powell arrived early for the meeting with George Carter. Brian arrived shortly after and showed him upstairs to the Drawing room. It was an elegantly furnished room, with clusters of finely carved chairs and sofas around coffee tables. There were expensive looking rugs on the floor and fine paintings on the walls. The rich drapes helped confirm a feeling of luxury. It was not a place one could imagine being tainted by violence. Carter should feel perfectly relaxed.

A handful of people were sat around drinking tea and coffee. On closer inspection, Powell realised they were all male and he doubted anyone was under fifty years of age. Certainly no one seemed to offer any potential threat. Powell chose an empty table with two seats by the windows, overlooking Pall Mall.

Brian took a newspaper from a side table and went to sit at a different table. As he passed a waiter, he ordered coffee. Although Powell didn't expect any trouble inside the club, Brian had volunteered to stay around just in case. He blended in perfectly with the other men in the room.

When the waiter approached, Powell also ordered some coffee. It would help pass the time until Carter arrived. Powell waited patiently and regularly glanced at the clock on the wall to check the time. He wasn't surprised Carter arrived five minutes late, no doubt thinking he was making a statement about who was most important.

Carter was alone when he entered the room, glanced around and spotted Powell sitting alone at the table. Powell raised his finger to signify he was the man Carter was due to meet. Carter didn't hesitate and walked directly to Powell's table.

"Want something to drink," Powell said amiably.

"No. This isn't a social occasion."

"I suppose not."

"You asked to meet and I'm a busy man so what do you want?"

Powell took a sip from his coffee and showed no inclination to hurry. "As I said on the phone, I want to live in a warmer climate. For that I need some additional funds. I was thinking five hundred thousand pounds."

Carter stared at Powell and then broke into a laugh. "Are you mad? I'm not giving you that sort of money."

"I'm pleased to see we are only arguing about the amount not the principle."

Carter's expression quickly changed to animosity. "Don't get smart with me."

"Considering you tried to have me killed, I think I'm being very reasonable."

"You are speaking utter nonsense. I haven't tried to have you killed."

"I assure you our conversation isn't being recorded."

"You are still talking rubbish."

Powell thought Carter actually sounded quite believable. No one was better at telling a convincing lie than a politician. "What sum would you be willing to pay for my silence?"

"It would be worth something to stop your interference. You must promise never to see my wife again."

"Agreed," Powell replied, proving he could lie as good as any politician.

"I'm not going to haggle with you. One hundred thousand pounds. That's my final offer."

Powell pretended to think about it for a few seconds before replying. "Okay. One hundred thousand." He didn't believe Carter had any intention of ever paying the money. "I want the money in cash. There shouldn't be any paper trail."

"It will take me a little time to organise such a large amount of cash."

"How long do you need?"

"Forty eight hours."

"That's fine. I can start to make my holiday plans. I want your wife and children present when we hand over the money."

"What! We just agreed you won't see my wife again."

"Carter, I don't trust you. And I definitely don't like the company you keep. If Rose and the children are present then I don't believe you will try anything, which puts their life in danger. They are my security."

"What guarantee do I have you won't demand more money in the future?"

"I'm not greedy. I intend to disappear. I know if I don't keep to my end of the bargain, you have friends who will hunt me down."

"Where are we going to make the exchange?"

"I'll let you know one hour before the handover. Make sure you only bring your wife and children. I don't want to see anyone else. Is that all clear?"

"Crystal."

"Then I think our meeting is concluded. I'm going to stay and finish my coffee."

Carter's expression showed he didn't like being dismissed but after a moment he stood up and strode away without further comment.

Brian came over and joined Powell.

"He didn't look very happy," Brian stated.

"He wasn't but he agreed to pay me one hundred thousand pounds."

"He can afford it. He's worth millions."

"He didn't put up too much of a fight when I said Rose and the children had to be present at the handover."

"Good. When is the handover?"

"He needed forty eight hours."

Powell's phone vibrated to tell him he had a message. You weren't supposed to use them within the club so he had put it on silent. As expected, the message was from Jenkins.

Carter turned right out of the club and kept walking. He was on his phone but I couldn't hear anything he said. He seemed to be alone. Do you want me to follow him?

Powell replied with:

No. Grab a taxi as planned and text me when you're outside and we'll come out.

The plan was they would jump straight in the taxi and be away before anyone could take action. There would be no standing around on the pavement trying to hail a taxi and making themselves a target. Powell didn't believe they, whoever they might be, would have anything as sophisticated as snipers on roof tops.

CHAPTER TWENTY EIGHT

Brendan Cooley had checked in with a very bad tempered Chairman. Thinly veiled threats about his future use to the organisation were listened to in silence. He was a bit long in the tooth to be receiving lectures like a naughty schoolboy. It pissed him off but he wasn't about to risk further aggravating his employer, by debating who was responsible for the failure in Nottingham.

The customer was always right! At least until he was wrong and then there were only two options. Kill the customer, which wasn't generally good for business if word got about. Or skip town. He wasn't yet ready to skip town.

If he wasn't given time to do his own research on targets, then he had to rely on the information provided by those paying for his services. He was willing to take responsibility for his actions but he should have been better warned what to expect. The man he had fought in the kitchen, who he now knew to be called Powell, was a professional. He had seriously good fighting skills.

The Chairman had grumbled that Brendan's failure was now compromising a major operation. Powell had valuable information and was blackmailing the organisation. Brendan had one last chance to redeem his reputation. There was to be a meeting between Powell and George Carter, the MP who had recently been on the television, sprouting a load of bollocks about terrorists. Carter would have his wife and two children at the meeting. Everyone was to be terminated.

Brendan was tempted to ask, why the hell had he gone to all the trouble of recovering the two children, if he was now supposed to kill them? But he said nothing. Ours not to reason why seemed an appropriate thought. He wasn't so keen on the next line of the poem; Ours but to do and die. He had no intention of ending up dead.

Everything was made harder by the fact, he would only have one hour notice of the location. He would once again be unable to plan ahead. Powell had already proven to be someone not to be taken lightly so the large bonus offered by the Chairman was definitely appropriate. Brendan had been told Carter would be taking one hundred thousand pounds to the meeting, which was to be his bonus.

At least the Chairman had provided two capable resources, who were to be under his orders until the job was done. Their presence stacked the odds significantly in favour of a good result.

Powell, Jenkins and Brian had gone over the plan a hundred times. The most important part of the planning had been to come up with the right location. It had to be suitable both for what they needed to do but also somewhere there was no possibility of anyone innocent being harmed. They were not willing to save Rose and the children at someone else's expense.

They visited a couple of possible ideas before settling on their final choice; A small, derelict industrial estate in Wembley. It had once housed a thriving collection of businesses but one after the other they had gone bankrupt. How many people had seen their dreams crushed? It was a depressing landscape but perfect for their needs. Large signs announcing the land was available for redevelopment were pinned to the entrance gates. Brian obtained the keys on the pretence the government might be interested in buying the site.

It was a huge advantage being able to check out the location in advance of the meeting and ensure there were no nasty surprises waiting for them. It was going to be impossible for Carter to organise an ambush in the one hour time window.

The plan revolved around Carter letting Rose and the children carry the money to Powell's car but there was the distinct possibility Carter had no intention of handing over any money in the first place. And even if he did bring the money, he might baulk at the idea of letting Rose and the children make the handover. In that case, Powell was going to simply put Carter on the ground and force the family into his car. Force was the operative word because he was far from certain Rose would voluntarily get into the car.

Powell had heard from Samurai that he had completed his part of the plan. He had hacked into Carter's home computer and sent him an image of the speech, with the dire warning it would appear on the computer of everyone who mattered if he didn't follow the plan for the meeting. Powell could only imagine Carter's reaction but hopefully it would keep him cooperating. There were a million things could go wrong but it was the best plan they could conceive.

Jenkins and Brian were already in place when Powell phoned Carter with the post code and time of the meeting.

CHAPTER TWENTY NINE

Jenkins sent a message to Powell's phone announcing they might have company. From his vantage point looking out over the entrance to the estate, Jenkins could identify the black saloon driving slowly past and then returning two minutes later. He may have been lost but the driver was looking in the direction of the estate each time he went past.

There was still twenty five minutes until the actual meeting and it wasn't Carter's car. Most likely it was someone hoping to hijack the rendezvous. It was suspicious enough to merit sending the message to Powell.

Jenkins wasn't surprised a few minutes later when he saw the three men come through the gates. Two of the men were carrying large bags. The type used to carry sports equipment but equally useful for transporting weapons such as rifles and grenade launchers. Jenkins recognised the men. They were the same ones from Alton Towers.

The men moved quickly, heading directly for the first building. All the time, their eyes were darting around looking for signs of anyone else present. They kicked through the wooden doors of the building and entered. They were now two floors below Jenkins, who had started to move the second he saw them head towards his building.

Jenkins hurried to the fire escape at the back of his building. Much as he wanted revenge on the men downstairs, it was more important the meeting went according to plan. He had checked the exits earlier and by the time the three men were climbing the stairs to the first floor, he was already out of the building.

He ran to Powell, who was two blocks away, sitting behind the wheel of a black London taxi cab, which had been provided by Brian. MI5 had a pool of the black cabs. With more than twenty thousand identical black cabs operating in London, they were perfect for surveillance operations.

The cab was parked down the side of a building and out of sight of anyone entering the estate so the intruders were so far unaware of their presence.

"There are three of them," Jenkins said, as he joined Powell in the front of the cab. "I'm pretty sure they are the same three from Alton Towers. Two of them were carrying large holdalls so they could have some heavy firepower."

"Could be worse odds."

"Did Brian get in touch?" Jenkins asked.

"Yes. They are all on the way." Brian was watching Carter's house and had messaged to say the whole family was in the car. There was no point in having the meeting if Carter didn't bring Rose and the children."

"We have twenty minutes," Powell said, checking his watch. "We need to neutralise them before Carter arrives."

"I was hoping you were going to say that. I owe them for a very sore head."

Earlier in the day, a bike courier company had delivered their weapons to the bar. Powell was very pleased Tina had ignored his concerns and sent the guns anyway. They were going to be needed. It was a pretty good guess, the three unwelcome visitors weren't carrying their lunch in the large holdalls.

"We need to be able to get behind them. Is that possible?" Powell queried.

"We can go back in through the fire escape. They will have eyes on the front of the building waiting for us and Carter to arrive."

"Good. Let's go."

Jenkins led the way back to the fire escape with Powell following. They crouched low and kept close to the side of the buildings as a precaution. Powell hoped it was them who were going to have the element of surprise on their side and they hadn't been detected.

Jenkins stopped at the top of the fire escape and peered inside the building. Satisfied it was safe, he slowly pulled open the door and entered with Powell close behind. They were in a long corridor with doors to either side.

They could hear voices up ahead. Powell nodded to indicate for Jenkins to follow him into the first office.

"It sounds as if they are in the main office, overlooking the road," Jenkins whispered.

"We have to go in fast and hard," Powell replied. "I've seen these guys work and they don't mess about. When we go through the door, you go left and I'll go right. If we can get the drop on them, we give them one chance to give up without a fight."

"They aren't here for the office party. I don't think there is a cat in hell's chance of them surrendering. And they will probably have had automatic weapons in those bags. Are you sure you don't want to just go in firing?"

"It would be good to take one of them alive, if possible," Powell replied. "We might learn who the fuck is behind all of this and get some solid evidence against Carter. But don't take any risks. Shoot to kill at the first sign of resistance."

"Okay. It's your call."

Powell led the way down the corridor. He was familiar with the building's layout, having checked out all the offices earlier. The large open plan office overlooking the road was empty of any furniture. There would be no cover once through the door but that also applied for the gunmen inside. Powell hoped they would have surprise on their side and it would be enough to compensate for being outnumbered.

Powell's heart was pounding as he came close to the voices. His senses were heightened by the knowledge of the danger that lay ahead. In a few seconds, he would be stepping into the unknown. Afina flashed into his mind. Now was not the time for getting himself killed. He forced himself to concentrate on the job in hand. He needed to remain fully focused. Any lack of concentration could prove to be fatal.

The door to the office was open and the voices were now loud enough for Powell to understand what was being said. One man was stressing the importance of killing everyone. Powell wondered if he had heard correctly. Was the man including Carter and the children in his orders to kill everyone?

Powell reached the office and flattened himself against the wall. Jenkins did the same. There was no point in hanging around. Powell looked at Jenkins and held his hand in the air. He counted down on his fingers from three to one.

Powell burst through the door, moving to the right. His arms were extended and his gun gripped in both hands. Jenkins followed close behind on his heels and moved to the left.

"Don't move," Powell shouted.

It was a futile order as the gunmen were already reacting to the surprise intrusion. One man was turning from the window and raising his assault rifle. Powell fired at the man but missed as the gunman was twisting sideways. Powell could hear further shots erupting from Jenkins gun at his side but his attention was still on the first man, who was now firing wildly from the ground without aiming.

The bullets passed overhead and crashed into the wall. Powell went down on one knee to reduce the target for the gunman and fired two shots himself. The gunman screamed as a bullet tore into his thigh. Out of the corner of his eye, Powell had seen there was only one other man in the room. Where the hell was the third gunman?

Powell returned to the gunman he had shot. He was raising himself off the ground and taking aim with his weapon. It was one of the men who had posed as a BT employee. Didn't he know when he was beaten? He was too dangerous to mess with. Powell put two shots into the chest of the man, who dropped his weapon and slumped sideways.

Powell swung around to his left and joined in firing at the last man still standing. The gunman refused to fall and Powell realised he was wearing a bullet proof vest. Powell switched his aim to the gunman's legs but before he could fire, the gunman was toppling to the ground. Jenkins had shot him through his left eye.

Powell stood surveying the room for a few seconds, looking for further signs of danger but none of the gunmen were moving. It was all over in less than a minute. He breathed in deeply and exhaled slowly. The adrenaline started to subside.

Jenkins walked to the first one he'd shot and kicked him hard in the ribs. The gunman didn't react. He then walked to the gunman Powell had shot. He repeated the kick to the ribs. Again there was no reaction.

"Where the hell is the other man?" Jenkins asked.

"Just what I was thinking. The Irishman is missing. Perhaps he went for a piss. We better go check."

The toilets were at the other end of the building to the fire escape. They approached cautiously, one of them down each side of the corridor. When they reached the toilet door, Jenkins lay on the ground. Powell stood to the side of the door and kicked it open. Jenkins was ready to fire but there was no one inside. They then repeated the search of the ladies toilet with the same negative result.

"We better take a look downstairs but I suspect he's scarpered," Powell said.

They searched the two lower floors but there was no sign of the Irishman.

"We need to get ready for Carter," Powell said, once they had returned to the room with the two dead bodies. "I'd better get back to the taxi. Then I'll give Brian a call and see how he wants to handle this mess."

"What if Carter was expecting to hear from these men, to confirm it was safe to meet? Surely the Irishman will have warned him off meeting?"

"From what I overheard them say, I think they were planning to kill everyone, including Carter and his family. The Chairman's patience must have finally run out. So I doubt they had arranged any call. The Irishman may believe we are in place to kill Carter, which would be doing him a favour. Anyway, I guess we'll know soon enough if Carter doesn't turn up."

"The extra fire power will come in useful," Jenkins suggested, picking up one of the rifles. "This is good gear."

"Just be careful where you shoot," Powell warned with a smile and left.

CHAPTER THIRTY

Brendan had been checking out the second floor of the building, wondering if it offered a better view of the kill zone, when he heard the sound of gunfire and falling bodies coming from the floor above. The shots were muffled by silencers but he had no doubt a firefight was taking place.

When everything went quiet, he assumed his men had been killed. If Powell and his friends had laid an ambush then they would have observed three men entering the building. They would be hunting for him very shortly.

He hurriedly retraced his steps to the car, which involved running across open ground from the building to the entrance to the estate. He didn't like the idea but had little choice. He made it safely back to the car, which was parked down a small side road, close to the entrance to the estate. He sat behind the wheel and breathed deeply. Had they walked into a trap? His best guess was both sides were planning to ambush the other but Powell and his friends had been in position first.

He thought about calling the Chairman to tell him he had once again failed. Fuck! He really didn't want to do that. Had he lost his edge? Failure was a new experience and not one he liked. He might have to think about retirement. It seemed a better option than telling the Chairman he'd messed up again. He had an exit strategy. He was a wealthy man and had everything necessary to disappear.

He brought his mind back to the present. There was no way he could hang around and try to kill Carter and his family. It was too dangerous. Should he warn Carter not to come to the meeting? No. Carter might question what he was doing there in the first place.

His best and only option was to complete the assignment. He now had a file on Powell with details of where he lived and worked. It was time to pay a visit to Brighton. Once he had dealt with Powell, he could tackle Carter and his family if they remained alive.

Carter drove through the entrance to the estate and parked in front of the first office building as instructed. Jenkins messaged Powell to inform him of Carter's arrival.

Powell arrived in his black cab a few minutes later. He stopped fifty feet from Carter's car. He stepped outside the cab and waited for Carter to get out of his car.

"Did you bring the money?" Powell asked when Carter climbed out of his car. He wasn't holding any bag.

"It's in the car."

"Then have Rose and the children bring it over to me."

Carter opened the rear door of the car and leaned inside. A moment later the children climbed out of the back and Rose stepped out of the front passenger door. She was carrying a briefcase.

"Send them over," Powell instructed. "You remain where you are."

Rose turned to her husband for guidance and he threw his hands in the air in a forward motion, to indicate they should go ahead. Rose walked to the front of the car and waited for her children to catch up. She smiled at them both in encouragement and they all started walking towards Powell. The children seemed perfectly relaxed as they knew and liked Powell.

Rose was about a metre from Powell when there was an explosion of gunfire ripping up the ground in front of George Carter, who dived behind the safety of his car. Rose seemed unable to comprehend what was happening until further bullets cut into the grass verge not far from where she was standing.

Powell grabbed Rose by the arm and shouted, "Quickly! Get in the cab."

Rose screamed and grabbed her children, pushing them into the back seat of the cab.

"Stay down," Powell ordered and then slammed the door shut.

A further series of shots rang out and tore into Carter's car, dissuading him from moving.

"Is this your doing?" Carter shouted out, looking in Powell's direction.

"These are your men. Not mine." Powell shouted back angrily. "I came here alone."

"So did I."

"I don't believe you," Powell screamed.

More shots were fired in both Powell and Carter's direction.

Powell took out his gun and fired a few random shots towards the building.

Two objects clattered down on to the road. Smoke started billowing out from the smoke grenades. Powell decided it was time to move.

He ran around the cab and jumped into the driver's seat. He put the car into reverse and sped backwards. The smoke was completely obscuring any clear view of the road or buildings.

Further shots were still being fired in Carter's direction.

Powell swung the cab around and took the next turning along the side of the building where earlier he had been parked up waiting for Carter to arrive.

CHAPTER THIRTY ONE

The smoke had cleared just a little as the black cab accelerated down the road. George Carter had been pinned down behind his car by the shots fired from the office but suddenly all fire was directed at the cab. He took his chance and jumped into the driver's seat of his car, keeping his head down low.

Before Carter could drive away, there was a large bang as the cab careered off the road and into the side of a building. After a moment there was a huge explosion and the cab erupted into flames.

Carter seemed cemented to the spot with shock. He stared through the clearing fog and could just about make out the body in the front passenger seat. It felt like he was watching a scene from a movie rather than real life. His brain couldn't process the information it was being fed by his eyes. Rose had been sitting in the front of the cab. Nobody could escape the flames.

Bullets spitting into the ground in front of his car, brought him back to reality. There was nothing he could do to help Rose and the children. He was convinced they were beyond help. He needed to get away or he would also end up dead.

Carter put the car into gear and his wheels screeched as he over accelerated. He did a U-turn and sped back towards the entrance to the estate, not stopping to check the road he joined was clear. He kept glancing in his rear view mirror to check he wasn't being followed.

He drove well above the speed limit until he was far enough away from the estate to believe he was safe. His brain was still struggling to come to terms with what he'd seen. Simon and Imogen had been in the back of the cab. They would have had no chance. They must be dead. No one could have escaped that fire.

His body started shaking as he thought of them trapped in the car, burning to death. Perhaps they were already unconscious when the fire took hold. He prayed they hadn't suffered. It had all happened so quickly there was nothing he could have done to help.

Who the fuck was responsible? It hadn't been Powell. He was driving the cab and also trapped in the flames. Someone had been trying to kill everyone present including Powell. Ultimately, it was all that bloody woman's fault. Rose was responsible for killing Simon and Imogen. He cursed the day they met.

Carter had only told one person the location of the meeting. The Chairman had insisted he called with the details of the meeting, the moment he heard from Powell. He had done as instructed and the Chairman must have sent someone to assassinate them all. He wanted to get rid of all evidence.

What kind of man could order the murder of two young children? Only a madman. What the hell was Carter going to do? Who could he trust? He knew who he couldn't trust.

He returned home and once through the door, helped himself to a large measure of whisky. He downed it in one and refilled his glass. He took the glass and went into the living room, where he slumped into an armchair. He couldn't get the images of the burning cab out of his mind.

He felt himself being enveloped by a sense of panic. What should he do next? He had to prepare himself for a visit from the police. He was going to have to act surprised when they told him his family were dead. How the hell was he going to do that? He wasn't a bloody actor. A couple more whiskeys and he wouldn't even be coherent. Perhaps that would be a good thing. His mind was jumping all over the place. How long would it take them to identify the bodies in the cab? When could he expect a visit from the police?

Perhaps he should contact the police first and accuse Rose of once again abducting the children? That wasn't a bad idea. He could accuse her of having an affair with Powell. That would explain finding their bodies together in the cab. If he hadn't heard from the police by the evening, he would contact them.

As a matter of routine, the police were also bound to ask about his whereabouts. He needed an explanation of where he had been today. He would just say he was at home. He couldn't come up with any better alibi. What if the police questioned his neighbours? He may even have been seen driving away from the house with Rose and the children.

In the space of a very short time, his life had become very complicated. The Chairman knew where he lived. What if he sent someone around to finish off the job? Carter jumped up from his chair and hurried to the windows. There was no sign of anyone loitering around outside.

He had to steady his shaking hand as he tried to pour a third whisky. The house suddenly seemed very quiet and empty. It would never again be filled with the sound of the children's laughter. He looked at the photos of his children on the wall and felt sick. He rushed to the toilet and threw up. Even when his stomach was empty, he stayed on his knees bent over the toilet bowl. Tears were running down his cheeks.

He slowly climbed to his feet. He splashed water on his face and looked in the mirror. He needed to get a grip. Nothing would bring the children back. He was a prominent figure, especially since his speech after the terrorist attack. The death of his family would be major news. It might even be considered a terrorist attack. Perhaps he had been identified as a target because of the speech he gave.

There would be huge sympathy for his loss. The Prime Minister was a walking disaster and the party were in turmoil. His star had been shining brightly recently and if he reacted the right way to this personal tragedy, it could propel him into number ten. After all, it was the attack on the Falkland Islands and Thatcher's response which transformed her reputation.

He needed to speak to the Chairman and point out the reality of the situation. Given the Chairman's support, the organisation could find itself with not only the President of the United States in power but also the British Prime Minister. Unfortunately, he couldn't just call the Chairman. He neither knew his name or his phone number. His only means of contact was by email.

Carter decided he would contact the Chairman and act as if he didn't believe the Chairman was implicated in the attack. Possibly the deaths of Rose and the children were an accident. Maybe the gunman was just trying to kill Powell. He wasn't to know the cab would burst into flames. That explanation made more sense. He would compose an email assuming it was an accident. In fact, he would go and do it immediately.

CHAPTER THIRTY TWO

It was four hours after the attack when Carter heard his front door bell chime. There were two men wearing suits stood at the door. He was nervous about answering but the Chairman had assured him of his full support. Carter didn't believe the two men were here to kill him but was still nervous as he opened the door.

"Mr. Carter, I'm Detective Inspector Green." The man held up his police identification. "Can we please come in and speak with you?"

"Of course. What about?"

"It would be best indoors."

Carter stepped back inside the house and fully opened the front door. He then led the two men into the lounge. "Can I get you anything?"

"No thanks," both men replied in unison.

"So what is this about?" Carter repeated.

"Let's all sit down," DI Green suggested.

Carter took the armchair and the two other men sat on the sofa.

Carter realised the man with DI Green hadn't been introduced. He didn't look like Green's junior and he was studying Carter. Perhaps he was there to assess Carter's reactions when the bad news about his family was delivered.

"Do you know the whereabouts of your wife and children?" DI Green continued.

"Why are you asking?" Carter replied.

"The bodies of a woman and two children have been found in a vehicle in North London. A man who was driving the vehicle has been taken to hospital."

Carter's expression of shock was real. He hadn't thought there was any possibility Powell could survive the car fire. "And you think the bodies are Rose and the children?"

"I'm afraid we do. We managed to get a fingerprint from the woman in the car and it was a match for your wife. We had her fingerprints on file from a traffic offence some years back."

"But what were they doing in North London?" Carter asked.

"We were hoping you could tell us that," DI Green responded.

"I've no idea. They went shopping but I didn't ask where exactly they were going." Carter was aware he might not be showing enough of a reaction. "Are you positive it's them?"

"It will take dental records for a positive identification of the two children but given it was your wife in the car..." DI Green didn't bother finishing the sentence.

Carter nodded his head from side to side in disbelief. "It can't be them. They were here only a few hours ago." He put his hand to his face to brush away the tear falling down his cheek. "What happened? Were they in an accident?"

"We are not at liberty at this time to speculate on the cause of death."

"What do you mean?" Carter pushed. "Why can't you tell me what happened? I'm an MP. I demand to know what happened."

The man sitting beside DI Green spoke for the first time. "I can tell you their death was not an accident. We are treating it as murder."

"Murder!" Carter exclaimed. "Was it terrorists?"

"We don't believe terrorists are responsible." The man with no name replied.

"I didn't get your name?" Carter probed.

"I didn't give it but just call me Brian."

"Are you a police officer?" Carter questioned.

"I work for the government," Brian explained. "I'm here because of concern your life might be in danger."

"Do you really think so?"

"It is a distinct possibility. DI Green will leave us now and we can discuss what actions are necessary to ensure your safety."

"I can see myself out," DI Green said, rising from his chair.

Carter paid no attention to the departing police officer. His focus was on Brian, who surely had to work for MI5. Brian probably wasn't even his real name. Carter liked the idea of getting protection from MI5. It might come in handy if the Chairman had any further doubts about his value to the organisation.

Brian waited for the sound of the front door closing before speaking. "Now he's left we can get down to business." The change in Brian's tone caused Carter to sit up a little bit straighter. "You do realise you were lucky to get out of there alive?"

Carter was shocked by the change in direction of the conversation. "What do you mean?" he blustered.

"Don't lie to me," Brian warned.

"Who are you?" Carter questioned.

"That's not important. Right now, I'm the only person between you and prison. And in or out of prison, I don't fancy your chances of staying alive very long once the Chairman finds out you have been arrested."

Carter was shocked to hear mention of the Chairman. How did the authorities know of his existence? Did it all come back to what Rose had discovered or had they known all along about the Chairman's plans and who was involved?

After a few seconds of silence to allow his words to sink in, Brian continued, "You have only one way out of this mess you've created. Tell me everything. If you do, then we can protect you." Having dangled the bait, Brian waited to see Carter's reaction.

Carter's mind was racing. He needed to calculate what was fact, admissible in a court of law, and what was pure circumstantial supposition. He started with, "I don't have any idea what you are talking about."

Brian looked Carter in the eyes without saying anything. Then he brought down his fist hard on the coffee table in front of the sofa. The crash reverberated around the room. "Look, you arrogant, brainless, moron. You are too stupid to play games with me. You haven't even asked who was driving the bloody car."

Carter realised he had made a mistake. The whisky was dulling his brain. He didn't ask because he knew it was Powell. "I assumed it was a taxi. My wife didn't take her own car."

"So your wife and children left here in a taxi?"

"Yes."

"Don't lie to me. I watched you drive out of here with your wife and children in the car. I'm sure once we start searching the traffic cameras, they will show you driving to Wembley."

"I'm not going to be intimidated by your aggressive attitude," Carter said uncertainly, finding a little bravado from somewhere. "I'm a Member of Parliament."

"That doesn't count for shit when you're involved in terrorism. You are a traitor to your country."

"You have no evidence."

"I don't think you fully understand the position you are in. If you don't tell me what I want to know, then I will set the wolves on you. They don't like traitors or terrorists. Believe me. You will answer *their* questions."

"You are just trying to scare me. Even MI5 have to keep within the law."

"Who said anything about MI5? This is the sort of work we subcontract. Mind you, the people interrogating you are likely to be ex MI5 or SAS. The type of people who have given service to their country and have no qualms about doing what is necessary to extract information from a terrorist."

"I am not a terrorist," Carter replied indignantly.

"What are you then? Tell me. You knew someone was going to commit an act of terrorism and did nothing. That makes you no better than a terrorist."

"You don't understand anything. We are not the terrorists. We are committed to fighting terrorism."

"Then we are on the same side. Tell me who is the Chairman and how do you intend to fight terrorism?" There was scepticism in Brian's voice. He was intrigued by Carter's claim to be fighting terrorism. He had thought it more likely Carter was mixed up in something for financial gain but there was the possibility he had a more idealistic agenda.

"I want to see my lawyer," Carter stated firmly and folded his arms.

"Do you think I am bluffing? I'm losing my patience. What is it to be? Are you going to talk to me or my more persuasive friends? They are waiting outside."

Carter had no doubt Brian's friends existed. Neither did he doubt their methods would not be to his liking. The Chairman may pose a threat but he had more immediate problems. He had to buy himself time.

"Well…" Brian prompted.

"I know very little. Everything is done on a need to know basis."

"Start at the beginning. Who is the Chairman?"

"I don't know. I've never met him in person. I receive instructions via email."

Brian was becoming angry. "This is complete bullshit. You didn't one day wake up and decide to start following random instructions you received by email. How did you first become involved in this so called fight against terrorism?"

"I was approached by a banker friend. He explained a group of very wealthy and influential people had come together to fight terrorism and poverty. They believed I shared their values so they wanted to help my career."

"I've seen the play."

"What do you mean?"

"Faust. Out of self-interest a man makes a pact with the devil. It didn't work out well for him either."

Now that Carter was talking, Brian was ready to hand him over to the experts for a full debrief. He picked up his phone and sent a very brief message. Then he walked to the front door before returning to his chair.

A few seconds later two men walked into the house. They had short haircuts and square jaws. Their muscles were evident despite their suits. They stood to attention awaiting instructions, rather like they were on a parade ground.

"These men are going to take you somewhere safe," Brian explained. "Someone else will come and ask questions. Answer them truthfully. If they suspect for a minute you are holding back, these men will make you tell the truth. Do you understand?"

Carter was holding his head in his hands. He said nothing but weakly nodded his agreement. Brian didn't expect they would have any trouble getting answers to their questions. In one short day, Carter's world had come crashing down. He had lost far more than his family. He had lost hope.

CHAPTER THIRTY THREE

The Chairman waited impatiently to receive confirmation from the Irishman that Carter's meeting with Powell had gone according to plan. Eventually, he received an email from Carter, with a brief update saying his family and Powell were dead. Carter didn't know who was responsible and was asking what to do.

The Chairman hoped he would still hear from Brendan or one of the other men on the payroll but the lack of contact eventually led the Chairman to believe they must either be in police custody or dead. He hoped it was the latter. Whatever the reality, there was no trail leading back in his direction. Even the Irishman just knew him as a voice at the end of the phone.

While he thought about what to do next, he sent Carter a holding email telling him he would investigate and be back in touch, as soon as possible. He didn't like communicating by emails. It might be secure but he preferred to look in a man's eyes when discussing something important. If he could have stood in front of Carter, he would know if he was telling the truth. Had he in some way engineered the meeting to his own advantage? It was unlikely but all possibilities had to be considered.

The Chairman could see some mileage in Carter's assertion, the loss of his family could further promote his career. But what sort of man lost his children and in the next breath wanted to take advantage of their death? It left a bad taste in the Chairman's mouth. He recognised his own driving ambition but Carter took it to a whole new level. The Chairman had to balance his personal disgust for the man with the potential he brought to the organisation.

He made some phone calls and set wheels in motion to try and establish whether the police did have his men in custody. It seemed odd that they had so messed up. They were meant to be the best professionals money could buy.

His next call was to a specialised contact, who could acquire him a new team. He wanted a team of six. Money was almost no object. They had to be the best. In particular, he needed a leader he could trust to execute the next part of the plan to improve the image of the President. The Irishman was to have carried out the failed assassination attempt in the coming weeks. Someone else would now have to take his place. Of course, he didn't share that information with the man at the end of the telephone. He just stressed he needed the best of the best.

The Chairman sat at his desk and considered his options. He needed to make a further call. The Englishman who occupied a seat at his top table needed to be made aware Carter was a potential risk. He should be given the chance to express his view. He also may need to cover his tracks.

Carter found himself bundled into the back of a Jaguar with tinted windows and driven at speed away from his home. He asked where they were going but was met with silence. At least the journey gave him some time to gather his thoughts. He began to contemplate what lay ahead. There was no evidence of his involvement in terrorism. He hadn't asked to be sent the speech.

After about half an hour, the man in the front passenger seat turned around and held out a black hood. "Put this on," he ordered.

Carter did as instructed and was enveloped in darkness. They had been heading down the M40 out of London and were close to Reading.

After a further twenty minutes of driving the car pulled to a stop. Seconds later the rear door was opened and someone grasped his shoulder and pulled him out of the car. He felt both arms gripped as he was frogmarched down what seemed like a pebbled path. He heard what he assumed was a front door close loudly behind him and shortly after he was pushed down into a chair. His hood was removed, he blinked and took in his surroundings.

He was in what seemed like a country cottage. One that looked like it belonged to a very old couple who hadn't changed the decoration in many years. He was in what had probably been the living room but the furniture was out of place. As he looked around he could see cameras high up in each corner of the room.

He was sitting in a very solid, wooden dining chair rather than an armchair. But it wasn't an ordinary dining chair. He could see the straps on the arms and glancing down saw there were similar straps around the chair legs. For good measure the chair legs were bolted to the floor. This was not a chair for eating meals. He swallowed nervously. At least the two men had not fastened him to the chair. Then again, why would they? He wasn't going anywhere. Not with the two heavies acting as babysitters.

The door opened and a woman in her early thirties entered. He felt a sense of relief. She had short blonde hair and a slim figure. She took a chair from the side of the room and placed it a couple of feet in front of where he was sitting.

"You can leave us," she said to the two heavies, who then did as instructed.

At least the immediate threat of physical violence had been removed. It made Carter relax a little. Although the two heavies would be just outside the door and others would be watching proceedings through the cameras.

"Mr. Carter or may I call you George?" She asked with a smile. She had perfect white teeth, blonde hair and spoke with a middle class, southern accent.

"George is fine."

"Good. My name is Sarah. I need to ask you some questions."

"My family has just been murdered and in all honesty, I'm not feeling great but I'll do my best." It was a ploy he decided to use while in the car. They couldn't expect him to be entirely compos mentis after what he'd been through.

"I'm very sorry for your loss," Sarah said without any real

sympathy. "The sooner I get answers to my questions, the sooner you can go home."

"Ask away."

"It's always best to start at the beginning."

"There isn't much to tell, really. I was approached by John Barnes, my banker friend, and asked if I wanted to join a philanthropic group of wealthy men looking to make a difference in the world."

"When was this?"

"About eighteen months ago."

"So who are these men?"

"I don't know. They all wanted to protect their anonymity. They weren't in it to be recognised for their good deeds."

"I'm sure they weren't," Sarah replied sarcastically. "So why don't you take me through everything that has happened since you received the invitation from Barnes."

The detailed questions came thick and fast and went on for what seemed like hours. Often the same question was phrased in two different ways. Carter was too experienced a politician to fall into their simple traps. Ten years of dealing with the press every day, prepared you to handle any form of interrogation.

"What can you tell me about events in Nottingham?" Sarah asked. "Who was the man who broke into the property where Rose and the children were staying?"

"I've no idea. I did use a bit of influence to have social services try and recover my children from Nottingham. I didn't think they were safe with Rose but that was all I did. I know nothing of any break in. I wouldn't want to put my children's lives in danger. It's possible the Chairman organised the break in but it had nothing to do with me."

"How very convenient," Sarah replied.

"What do you mean?"

"To blame the mysterious Chairman for everything. However, you can't actually tell me anything about this Chairman. You can see how it looks from my perspective."

"I'm telling the truth," Carter stressed.

"Let's move on. How do you explain a copy of the speech you gave being on your computer, the day before the terrorist attack?"

"It wasn't. It must have been a computer glitch. Something wrong with the date."

Carter looked Sarah in the eye. Her facial expression didn't show what she was thinking. Did she believe what she was hearing?

"Of course. I should have thought of that. A computer glitch. The bane of all our lives."

Carter smiled. "I've never been very good with technology. Don't understand the damn stuff."

Sarah smiled back at him. "I know what you mean… Tell me again about events today in Wembley. Who were the men doing the shooting?"

"I've told you. I have no idea." Carter didn't like the way the damned woman kept jumping back and forth. He had already answered these questions.

"Make an informed guess."

"Terrorists probably. Perhaps they were targeting me and my family because of my speech."

Sarah paused with the questions. She stood up. "We aren't making the progress I would have liked. Is it because I'm a woman? Are you not taking me seriously?"

Carter was surprised by the change in direction. "I'm telling you everything I know."

Sarah stepped forward and delivered a sharp slap to Carter's face. "I understand you like to beat up on women."

"That's not true."

"Does it turn you on? Is it how you get your kicks?" She tried to slap him again but he put up his hand to fend off the blow.

"Do you like it more when the woman resists? Did Rose resist?"

"I didn't hit my wife."

"Then how do you explain the many bruises?"

"She fell over."

"Of course she did… Send Dave and Harry in," Sarah said out

aloud.

Seconds later the two heavies entered the room.

"What are you going to do?" Carter asked nervously.

"Take off your clothes," Sarah instructed.

Carter looked aghast. "I won't."

"Take them off or I will have my friends do it for you."

Dave and Harry took a step nearer.

Carter slowly stood up. He removed his jacket. "You have no right to do this. You're breaking the law."

"George, I can assure you everything I do is perfectly legal. We have an order signed by the Prime Minister. Seems she isn't your biggest fan. Probably has something to do with you wanting her job."

"I'm a Member of Parliament. You can't…"

Sarah took a step closer and before he knew what was happening, delivered a punch to his solar plexus. "I don't give a fuck who you are. I didn't know Rose but I'm told she suffered severe beatings at your hand. It sounds like your parents didn't bring you up properly, George. Someone should have taught you not to hit defenceless women. Would you like to hit me? Of course not because you know I'm not defenceless. You know what that makes you, George?" Sarah put her face against George's ear. "That makes you a coward and a bully. I don't like either. Now take your clothes off while you are still able to do it by yourself."

Carter was bent over in pain. He was making small wheezing noises. He slowly straightened before removing his shirt and then his trousers. He was left in just his boxer shorts and socks.

"And the rest," Sarah ordered. "I suggest you take off your socks first. There is nothing worse than seeing a naked man standing in just his socks."

Carter removed his socks. He looked at Sarah, his eyes pleading not to have to remove his last item of clothing.

"Don't be bashful. I haven't got all day," Sarah cajoled. "There are approximately three and a half billion cocks on the planet. I don't suppose there is anything different about yours."

"Fuck you," Carter said and pushed down his boxers.

"That explains everything," Sarah said staring at his genitals. "It must be tough for a man to go through life with such a tiny excuse for a cock. Is that why you beat up Rose. Are you deep down ashamed you're not a real man?"

"I bet you're a dyke," Carter spat out.

"So small dick man does at least have some balls. Actually, I'm not a lesbian but we're digressing. Sit your little cock back down in the chair."

Carter obeyed and found the two heavies quickly using the leather straps to secure him to the arms and legs of the chair. The leather bit into his skin. For the first time since he arrived at the cottage, he wasn't sure he would ever get to leave.

"I am going to ask the questions again and this time I want better answers. If I don't like your answers… Well, we don't have to go into detail. I'm sure you get the idea."

CHAPTER THIRTY FOUR

Brendan had spotted Powell and another man returning home on the evening of the shootings in Wembley. He was parked up in his car a little way along the street from where Powell lived. Brendan had a good view of the house. It wasn't anything special. Certainly nothing like the house in Nottingham.

The other man carried himself like a soldier. Brendan realised he knew the second man. He had been looking after the kids in Alton Towers. Damn! They should have taken him out when they had the chance. Brendan would place a large bet he had been at Powell's side in Wembley. He was an added complication.

Brendan had no intention this time of acting before he was ready. He would choose the right moment rather than be pressured into acting faster than he liked. He would study his target and understand Powell's routines. If it took a few days, it wasn't a problem. Hopefully, the second man wasn't a permanent fixture in Powell's life and would only be visiting.

Brendan observed the lights in the house being turned off and shortly after, the two men emerged. They hadn't stayed home very long. Brendan followed them at a discrete distance to the bar Powell owned in the centre of Hove. Perhaps they were in need of a drink after a hard day. He would be having one later for sure.

Although Brendan didn't believe either man would easily be able to identify him from their earlier encounters, he wasn't going to risk entering the bar. He decided to drive back to the house and have a look around while it was empty.

Brendan checked the street was empty, then strode up to the side gate. It was bolted but he simply stretched his hand over the top of the gate and slid back the bolt. He found himself in a rear garden, which consisted mostly of a lawn and weeds around the edge in what was masquerading for flower borders. The grass looked in need of cutting. Powell obviously wasn't much of a gardener. There were a row of trees at the bottom of the garden, which stopped the house from being overlooked by the neighbour's house.

Brendan was surprised to find there was a kitchen window open. Powell obviously wasn't very bothered about security. Perhaps he wasn't such a professional after all. Brendan hoped that wasn't true. He could explain away his failings on the basis he had encountered a finely tuned professional but not if he was just some amateur do-gooder.

Brendan realised he was starting to think about Powell differently to other assignments. Normally, it was just a target and a job that needed doing. This was becoming something else. It was more personal. Even if he wasn't being paid, he would want to finish this job.

Brendan accepted the invitation and climbed through the window. He was careful not to break anything as he didn't want Powell to know there had been a visitor. He went through each room in the house, searching for clues to give insights into Powell's life.

The living room was quite modern and one wall was decorated with family pictures. Brendan studied the array of pictures. There was a young Powell getting married and photos of a daughter at different ages growing up. He was quite the family man.

Brendan poked around in the drawers and cupboards but there wasn't much to discover. There weren't even any porno magazines or sex toys in the bedside tables. Powell did have an outfit hanging in his wardrobe that was revealing. It was a traditional outfit used for practising martial outfits. There was a black belt also attached. So, that confirmed Powell's skills. Not that they would do him any good next time they met. Brendan didn't plan to get close. A bullet would do the job.

After twenty minutes, Brendan decided he had seen enough. He left everything as he had found it and exited through the front door.

Leaving through the front door was less likely to attract attention from nosey neighbours than using the side entrance.

He walked straight to his car without seeing anyone. He needed a disguise. Nothing too elaborate. Normally he was clean shaven so growing a beard would be a good first step. He was already showing two days of stubble. He would also get hold of some glasses. He fancied looking like a college professor.

Brendan spent a sleepless night in his car waiting for Powell to return home but he never appeared. Perhaps he had a bed at the bar? Or maybe he liked to party with the pretty girls who he imagined worked in the bar. The other man had also not returned so perhaps they were both celebrating the events in Wembley. That thought troubled Brendan. Their celebrations would be short lived.

Brendan continued watching until mid morning but then his stomach told him, he needed to eat. He found a pub and ordered a pint of Guinness to go with fish and chips. It had been a while since he had a pint while on a job. He normally abstained while working.

He had been thinking of letting the Chairman know he was still in play. On the one hand, he could just do a disappearing act but he was going to kill Powell first no matter what. As he was only paid half of his fees up front, it would be best to get in contact if he wanted the remainder of his money when the job was done. He decided to send a brief message.

Feeling full, it was time to get back to work.

CHAPTER THIRTY FIVE

Powell had hurried to the bar with Jenkins, desperate to see Afina. Events in Wembley had reminded him of his mortality. It wasn't just that he now had more to live for but getting himself killed would be terribly unfair on Afina, having made her wait so long to get their relationship off the ground.

He had paid a quick visit to hospital to get a burn on his hand treated, which he'd received getting out of the car before it exploded. Otherwise, he was fit and well. He recognised if he kept up his current line of work, one day his luck would run out. He didn't want to think about someone having to tell Afina he wasn't coming home.

At the bar, Powell had briefly explained to a shocked Afina what took place at the meeting in Wembley. He then asked that they didn't speak about it again. He suggested Afina call Mara and invite her to join them for a drink to help keep Jenkins company. Powell was intent on doing a little bit of matchmaking, as Jenkins seemed far more willing to run into a room full of heavily armed killers, than invite Mara out on a date.

The atmosphere was more like a wake than a party and the four of them reminisced about the past and how they had all met. At the end of the evening, Jenkins had gone off in a taxi with Mara, supposedly to visit a club in Brighton but Mara had told Powell not to expect him back. He would be spending the night at her place. He just didn't know it yet.

Powell awoke feeling tired and with a bit of a hangover. Afina took the shower first as she needed to be downstairs to open the bar for breakfast. He realised going to bed with Afina at one in the morning wasn't the same thing as going to sleep at one. They were equally unable to leave each other alone when they reached the bedroom and it was at least an hour later before they thought of sleep.

The morning passed quietly with Powell having breakfast and doing some overdue paperwork in the office. About eleven, Jenkins reappeared and joined Powell at his table.

"Did you have fun?" Powell asked lightly.

"Brilliant night."

"Well?"

"Well what?"

"Did you and Mara…?"

"None of your damned business."

Afina hurried over to their table. "Do you need feeding?" She asked Jenkins.

"I'll have the full works please," Jenkins replied, referring to the name of the biggest breakfast on the menu.

"Knowing Mara, he probably already had the full works," Powell laughed.

Afina nodded her head furiously at Powell, scowled and walked away.

"What did I say wrong?" Powell asked. "I was just joking."

"No we didn't have sex," Jenkins said. "I couldn't."

Powell became serious. "Don't worry. It can happen to any of us after too much booze."

"That wasn't the problem. We had a great night and when we went back to her place, Mara wanted to make love but I messed things up."

"What happened?"

"I asked her how many men she had sex with last week. And whether she would be having sex with more men today."

"Oh! That probably wasn't a good idea. She's never hidden what she does for a living. But that's just her work. She doesn't share her feelings with her customers."

"I like her too bloody much. It would have driven me mad all day today, if I was thinking about her having sex with other men."

"You're thinking about it anyway."

"Yes. But it would have been so much worse if we'd..."

"Are you a virgin?" Powell asked.

"What sort of stupid question is that?"

"So you also have had sex with other partners?"

"It's not the same."

Powell decided it was best to change the subject. "What are your plans? Are you going to stick around a while or head back to Wales"

"I'll head off after I've eaten. If you don't need me for anything else?"

"No. There's nothing else. Thanks for your help. I'll transfer you some money later."

"That's not necessary. No one was paying you this time."

"Not exactly but I told Samurai to dip into Carter's account for some fees. I'm sharing them between us all." It was a lie but Powell wanted to pay Jenkins for his help.

"Well in that case... Thanks. That bastard Carter can afford to pay."

Jenkins ate his breakfast and said goodbye to Afina. Powell gave him a lift back to his house to collect his few belongings and pick up his car.

When Powell returned to the bar, Afina told him she had spoken with Mara, who was feeling a bit down.

"It's my fault," Powell admitted. "I was trying to push them together. I guess with what's happened between us, I wanted the same for Jenkins."

"Sometimes, men need a little time to recognise what's right for them," Afina said smiling. "He needs to work on Mara. He can't expect her to change her life in one night. He shouldn't give up. She doesn't plan to be an escort for ever."

"It's a nice day and I need some fresh air. Do you fancy going for a walk?"

"I could skive for a couple of hours this afternoon. Where are you thinking of going?"

"Let's walk along the sea front. I want to get a couple of things from the shops as well." Powell was keen to buy Afina a piece of jewellery. He wanted to give her a present. Something to mark their new relationship.

"I'll be free in about an hour. If that's okay?"

"That's fine. I'll have another coffee and read the paper."

CHAPTER THIRTY SIX

Powell and Afina decided they would walk from the bar along the seafront to Brighton, do some shopping and then take a taxi back to the bar. It was only a couple of miles.

"How is Adie getting on?" Powell asked.

"She's having fun. She regularly goes out with some of the others for drinks after work."

"She sure has grown up."

"I know. She told me yesterday she had sex with Tony the previous night."

"Tony?"

"Antonio. Works behind the bar. Dark, good looking and Spanish."

"I know who you mean. Isn't he a bit old for her?"

"He's twenty one."

"I hope she took precautions. I don't want your Mum blaming me for making her a grandmother."

"She's on the pill. And she wasn't a virgin. She's had a couple of boyfriends back home."

"Was Tony a casual thing or something more?"

"More I think. She likes him."

They had been holding hands as they walked. Powell stopped and pulled Afina in close. He moved his arms around her middle. "I'm so glad you didn't fall for Tony or any of the other good looking boys in the bar."

"That's the reason I didn't. They are mostly boys not men."

"I'm feeling my age recently," Powell admitted.

"Perhaps we should slow down at night," Afina smiled. "If I am being too demanding, you must tell me."

"You are not too demanding and I have no wish for you to change.

It's just things like, I remember when I started the bar, I wasn't much older than most of the staff. Now when I look around the bar, I feel positively ancient. And I'm wondering if I'm getting a bit old for the jobs I keep doing. I'm not as fast as I used to be."

"Then you had better train harder."

"It's bad enough for you I'm such an old git. I don't want you worrying about what I'm doing when I'm away."

Afina took on a serious expression. "Don't you dare," she threatened. "Don't you dare change anything about you. I, more than anybody, know the danger you put yourself in to help others. I'm not worried for you. I'm proud of you and what you do to help other people. It's the person you are. The person I love. I don't want to be with you if by being with you, I am changing you from being the person willing to risk anything to help those who need your help."

Powell could see Afina's eyes burning. He felt he could see right into her soul. She had meant every word she had said. "I love you," he said for the first time since they had become lovers.

"And I love you. But you know that. You've always known that."

Powell leaned close and kissed Afina lightly on the lips. As he went to pull away, she pulled him closer and kissed him deeply and passionately.

"I take back what I said about feeling old. When I'm with you, I feel twenty years younger."

"Good. Does that mean you might manage three times a night not just twice?"

Powell laughed. "I think it might."

As he took her hand to continue walking, he noticed the car pull up at the side of the road. He was permanently observing everything that went on around him, even the mundane. A man stepped out of the car. He was wearing sunglasses and had a baseball cap on his head. Powell turned back to Afina.

He heard someone cry out a warning and when he looked in the direction of the shouting, he saw the man who had stepped out of the car, narrowly avoid colliding with a bicycle. Tourist, Powell thought. He doesn't realise there is a biking lane along the seafront.

"Watch where you're fucking going," the man on foot called out.

Powell was stunned by hearing the broad Irish accent. He looked again at the man. He was the right age and build.

"Quickly," Powell said, pulling on Afina's hand. He knew his imagination was probably working overtime but started to drag her along the busy pavement.

"What's wrong?"

"Just a precaution," he answered. Fuck! He felt very vulnerable with Afina at his side. Powell glanced over his shoulder. The Irishman was following. Then again, he could just be heading into Brighton. He didn't seem to be paying them any special attention.

"Are we being followed?" Afina queried.

"I'm not certain."

Powell didn't believe the Irishman would want to gun them down in front of so many witnesses but he couldn't be certain. They were passing the burnt out West Pier and the new viewing tower. The moving observation tower was half way up the column. He couldn't see the fascination but the queue suggested plenty of people were interested in the views.

He pulled Afina across the main road and glancing behind was relieved to see no sign of the Irishman. Perhaps he had been planning to go up the tower. Powell relaxed a little. He was getting paranoid in his old age. Not every Irishman posed a threat. He slowed his pace and headed towards the town centre.

"Is he gone?" Afina asked.

"I think so." Powell gave a reassuring smile. "Sorry, I didn't mean to scare you."

"I wasn't scared. I'm with you." Afina smiled broadly.

"Thanks for the vote of confidence but …" Powell didn't finish the sentence because looking in the window of the hotel they were passing, he spotted the Irishman about twenty metres behind. He must have crossed the road earlier and was following them from the other side of the road. Powell had very obligingly crossed the road to make the Irishman's job easier. At least Powell didn't think he'd done anything to reveal he knew he was being followed. "Let's get a drink," he suggested.

"Is he still behind us?"

"I still don't know for sure if he's following us."

"A drink sounds good to me."

Powell led Afina into the Holiday Inn hotel. Once inside, he had a quick look back at the entrance and could see the Irishman walk past outside, without even a glance inside. "I think we'll skip the drink," he said, leading the way through the foyer, past a bar and out of the hotel's side entrance used by residents, who lived in the upper floor apartments. He'd once been to a party in one of the apartments.

Powell continued to hold Afina's hand as he led the way down the quiet side street, back to the seafront. Unfortunately it was a dead end in the other direction. On the corner of the main road, he came to a halt and took a look around the side of the hotel, to see if there was any sign of the Irishman. Despite seeing no sign of him, Powell had lost his appetite for going shopping. He didn't look behind as they started walking away from town and back towards the bar.

CHAPTER THIRTY SEVEN

Powell would have liked to jump in a taxi but none of the ones passing were empty and there was no taxi stand nearby. They decided to leave the seafront and walk up to Western Road, which led directly back to the bar but had the advantage of going past shops and other bars.

Powell liked to sample food and drink at other bars as it gave him a chance to judge his competitors and sometimes learn something that could improve his own bar. Feeling more relaxed, they stopped for a coffee and a slice of cake at a newly opened place. They placed their order and were told it would be brought to their table. They watched and waited for an age as the two people behind the counter spent more time chatting than preparing the food.

"How long do you think before they go bankrupt?" Powell asked.

"I hope you would fire me if I was so slow with a simple order," Afina answered. "They have no idea of the meaning of service."

Although Powell had originally offered Afina the job of waitress because he felt sorry for her and wanted to help, her subsequent climb to manager of the bar had been entirely down to her own hard work and aptitude for the job.

When Powell thought about Afina with his head instead of his heart, he recognised it would have been better for them both if they had never met. Afina had been subjected to terrible abuse as a trafficked sex worker. Powell was besotted with Afina but the relationship was tinged with a feeling of guilt. His daughter had paid a terrible price for him to find love.

The coffee and cake was good when it finally arrived. They shared the two different cakes they had ordered. He hated to think of the calories. He would need to work extra hard next visit to the gym.

They paid the bill and Powell made a point of leaving no tip. They glanced in a few shops windows on the way back to the bar but still arrived earlier than originally expected.

"Why don't we go upstairs?" Afina suggested. "It won't get busy for another couple of hours."

Powell smiled and was about to agree when the Irishman entered the bar. "You go ahead and I'll be up shortly," he encouraged, taking Afina by the arm and directing her towards the back of the bar.

"Okay but don't keep me waiting long. I don't want to have to start without you."

As Afina walked away, Powell turned to see the Irishman take a seat at a table. His presence certainly wasn't a coincidence. The Irishman seemed to be concentrating on the menu. He did glance up and cast his eyes at other tables but never in Powell's direction.

Powell thought about his actions in town. It could have looked natural when they entered the hotel. The Irishman hadn't known how long they would be there and perhaps decided to reacquire his target back at the bar, rather than follow him into the hotel. It was possible the Irishman didn't know he'd been spotted.

Powell watched out the corner of his eye as Afina's sister walked up to the table and took the Irishman's order. Why did it have to be Adie's table? Afina would never forgive him if she was to be hurt. At least she was upstairs out of harm's way. He breathed a sigh of relief when he watched her walk away again with the Irishman's order.

The Irishman was a cool bastard. Sitting there as if he didn't have a care in the world. What did he hope to achieve? Perhaps he was playing psychological games. Trying to unsettle his target. If that was his intention, he was bloody well succeeding.

There were other customers spread thinly around the bar. He surely wouldn't want to commit murder in front of so many witnesses. He should also have noticed the cameras in the bar. Everything would be recorded on CCTV. Only a fool or a madman would start something in the bar and the Irishman was neither. Powell had his gun in the office. He needed to fetch it and be prepared to confront the

Irishman.

Powell headed for the office, with a glance over his shoulder to ensure the Irishman wasn't following. He was showing no sign of moving.

Powell kept his gun in the safe behind his desk. He bent down to open the safe and was about to reach inside when he heard movement in the doorway.

"Keep your hands where I can see them," the Irish voice ordered.

Powell thought about grabbing the weapon and fighting back but knew it would be hopeless. How the hell had the Irishman moved so fast? There could be only one outcome if he didn't do as ordered. He lifted his hands high in the air and waited for the impact of the inevitable bullet. He cursed his stupidity. He had made it easy for the Irishman. Why didn't he just get on and pull the trigger?

"Have you got my hundred thousand pounds in that safe?" the Irishman asked.

"No. It's in the bank," Powell replied, now realising why he was still alive. His mind was racing, calculating if the Irishman's greed would stop him pulling the trigger.

"Pity. It would have made a nice bonus."

Powell sensed the Irishman was going to pull the trigger and there was nothing he could do about it.

"Brendan Callaghan," Powell stated. "Member of the Ulster Volunteer Force. Wanted for the murder of many innocent Catholic civilians. Now known to be living and working in the United States."

"So you've done your research. It doesn't matter. A couple of weeks from now, I will have a whole new identity. If you're a religious man, it's time to say a prayer."

There was something about the Irishman that didn't seem right but Powell couldn't put his finger on what it was. "Can I turn around?" he asked. "Or do you only shoot people in the back?"

"Feel free."

Powell slowly turned. He had to find reasons to keep Callaghan talking. Powell's face showed his shock.

Callaghan had his arm outstretched, pointing his gun at Powell's body. There was no chance of taking any defensive action, Callaghan was too far away.

"I can get you the money," Powell suggested.

"I don't think so." A small smile crossed Callaghan's lips and Powell knew life was about to end. He closed his eyes and awaited his fate. He prayed there really was an afterlife and he would shortly get to see his wife and daughter.

There was the sound of a shot from a silenced pistol and then a further shot. Powell felt no pain. He opened his eyes. Callaghan had fallen to the ground.

The Irishman, who Powell had seen follow him in town and was a short time ago, ordering food in the bar, walked forwards. Powell had been surprised when he turned around and found Callaghan was not the man from in town. It was an easy mistake to make. They had similar builds and the baseball hat had made it more difficult for identification. Powell's first thought had been the two men were working in partnership.

"You can put your hands down," the Irishman said. "I'm not here for you." He pulled Callaghan's body inside the office and closed the door.

"Who the hell are you?"

"Let's say I was on the other side to Brendan."

Powell took that to mean he was a member of the IRA, which also meant he used to be on the other side to Powell. "I suppose I should say thanks," Powell said.

"I suppose you should," the Irishman agreed. "This was personal for me. Brendan killed my son. That doesn't get forgotten, no matter how many years go by or what treaties get signed."

Powell felt exactly the same. He had found his wife's killers and exacted revenge. "How did you trace Brendan to here?" Powell asked, realising he was missing a piece of the jigsaw.

"We have a mutual acquaintance in MI5, who tipped me off Brendan might be coming after you. It was the first lead I had in almost twenty years so I didn't hang around."

"I thought you were after me in town,." Powell said. "Brian might have warned me about you."

"So you did spot me. I thought you might have. I was just following you in case Brendan turned up. I recognised him soon as I walked in your bar. When I saw him get up and follow you, I thought it was my chance as you seemed to be receiving all his attention. I arrived just in time."

"You certainly did."

The Irishman placed his gun on the table. "I won't be needing this. You seem pretty calm. Do I take it you have had guns pointed at you before?"

"I have but that was a bit too close for comfort."

"Were you in the same line of work as our mutual friend?"

"A long time ago."

"Ireland?"

"For a short time."

"They were bad days."

"They certainly were," Powell agreed.

"You should call your friend and sort out what happens to the body."

"Want a drink before you go?" Powell asked, taking a bottle of whisky from his desk drawer. There was a time, he would have thought it inconceivable he would share a drink with someone from the IRA. Life was getting weirder by the day. Powell would have to speak with Brian and find out more about the man who had saved his life. Had they ever crossed paths before?

"Don't mind if I do," the Irishman said.

Powell placed two glasses on the desk and filled both with a double measure. He handed a glass to the Irishman and they both downed their drinks in one without saying anything.

"Thanks," the Irishman said and without further ado turned and left the office.

Powell looked at the body on the floor. He had stood over far too many dead bodies over the years. Many of them cut short in the prime of their life. He was too accustomed to violence. Powell felt zero compassion for the dead Irishman. He had chosen his way of life. In Powell's experience of Ireland, the worst on each side enjoyed the violence they perpetrated. It had nothing to do with religion or politics. They were simply pathological killers. If all the money in the world spent on weapons was put to feeding the world, no one would ever go hungry.

Powell knew he was lucky to be alive. For a few seconds, his life had hung by a very fine thread. Perhaps it was written somewhere that it wasn't yet his time. Maybe the God of love had pulled weight and decided he and Afina deserved a chance at love. He poured himself another whisky and hoped it would be the last dead body he would see for a very long time. He didn't pretend to himself he would never see another one.

CHAPTER THIRTY EIGHT

Powell had invited Angela to come down to Brighton for lunch. It had been two weeks since Carter resigned, having cited his inability to continue with his career while suffering with the loss of his family. The press release said he needed a complete break from politics. People had been very sympathetic to his decision and it was wrongly assumed by many that after a period of mourning he would return to politics.

He had been so terrified by his interrogators, he had fully answered every question they posed. However, he didn't have a seat at the big table so he was of only limited use. There was no appetite in government to prosecute Carter and wash far too much dirty laundry in public. In reality, there was little evidence that would stand up in a court of law.

Carter was a broken man and had been told to keep a low profile and disappear from the public eye. He was left under no illusion what would happen to him if he didn't do as instructed. He was still a rich man and it was suggested he might prefer a warmer climate to England.

Having revealed John Barnes was the banker friend, who had introduced him to the Chairman's plans, Carter wasn't of much further use. He didn't know the name of the Chairman or his fellow conspirators. Barnes had explained it was a sensible precaution on the part of the Chairman to keep his identity secret. His name would be revealed only if Carter was invited to join the inner circle.

Barnes, who was a bastion of society, was a part of the inner sanctum and did know the Chairman's name. MI5 would be crawling all over Barnes' communications to establish the Chairman's name. They wanted to gather as much information as possible before confronting Barnes or doing anything about the Chairman.

Sarah had informed him, she was to be his new best friend and he wasn't to say or do anything without checking with her first. She wrote the resignation announcement and composed emails to the Chairman and Barnes, saying Carter couldn't face life after what had occurred.

Powell had invited Afina to join him and Angela for lunch. When he introduced her to Angela as his new girlfriend, he had received raised eyebrows from both women. Afina had only briefly, previously met Angela but their stories were well known to each other.

"It makes a change to hear some good news," Angela said, as they all sat down. "Congratulations to you both."

Afina was smiling broadly. "I can't believe Powell called me his girlfriend.

"You make a good couple," Angela said. "Rose and I didn't make very good choices in husbands but Powell is a good man."

"We both owe him everything," Afina said.

"You'll make me blush," Powell replied. "I hope you two aren't going to gang up on me."

"Last time we had lunch was at that restaurant in Covent Garden," Angela said. "Before I took you to meet Rose for the first time."

Powell had known the shadow of Rose and the children would hang over their lunch.

"How was the funeral?" Powell asked. Rose and the children had been buried ten days earlier. Powell had chosen not to attend as George Carter would be present, pretending to be the grieving husband.

"It was nice but terribly sad." A tear formed at the corner of Angela's eye. "When I think about those poor children… And that bloody man is walking around free. It's a disgrace."

"Trust me. It is for the best."

"It doesn't look that way to me. He should pay for what he did to Rose."

"I promise you, all is not as it seems. He's helping Brian's colleagues but I can't say any more than that and please don't quote me."

Angela didn't look convinced. "He's part of the establishment. His sort always get away with murder. Both literal and otherwise."

Powell smiled inwardly and didn't reply that most people would describe Angela as very much part of the same establishment. Before he could say anything further, their conversation was interrupted by Adriana delivering their food. Afina introduced her sister and the mood changed to more light hearted for a moment.

"We are going for a drive after lunch," Powell announced, once Adriana had departed.

"Where are we going?" Angela asked suspiciously.

"It's a surprise."

"I like surprises," Afina said enthusiastically. "Powell is full of them recently."

"Are you going to give us a clue?" Angela enquired.

Powell took a large mouthful of his sea bass and then used his hands to gesture he couldn't speak.

"Do you know where we're going?" Angela asked, turning to Afina.

"No idea," Afina replied with a shrug.

"Powell is looking a little tired," Angela remarked. "Have you not been letting him get any sleep?"

Powell almost choked on his fish.

Afina smiled broadly. "We are making up for lost time."

Powell finished his mouthful and drank some water to clear his throat. "Can we please change the subject?"

"Do you plan on having children?" Angela asked to Afina.

"I'm not sure," Afina replied with a glance towards Powell.

"You should do," Angela encouraged. "Powell is great with children."

"We've only just started going out," Afina explained.

"Practising is good fun," Angela said. "But don't wait too long. Powell isn't getting any younger."

"I am here you know!" Powell interjected.

"Where did you say you were taking us?" Angela asked with a smile.

"Perhaps I should go eat my lunch somewhere else?" Powell responded good naturedly.

"You win," Angela conceded. "I won't mention it again."

"Good. Let's enjoy the rest of our lunch."

CHAPTER THIRTY NINE

Powell drove the thirty minutes to Gatwick airport. As they came closer to the airport, both Afina and Angela were making guesses about their intended destination.

"Perhaps Powell is taking us on holiday," Afina joked. "I hope we are going somewhere nice."

"That would be a good idea," Angela agreed. "As long as he has organised someone to look after my children"

"Don't take this the wrong way," Powell replied. "But much as I love you both, there is no way I would consider going on holiday with you both. You would gang up on me too much."

"Angela, my English is not perfect. Did my boyfriend just insult us?"

"I think he did," Angela laughed. "But I'm sure it was aimed more at me than you."

"I'm not sure that's true. I think you are right, Powell is looking tired. How many nights do you think he needs to sleep by himself to get over his tiredness?"

"Not too many," Angela stressed. "He might get grumpy."

"That's what I mean about ganging up on me," Powell stressed. "You'd only take me to carry your bags."

"Are you saying we are such feeble women, we can't carry our own bags?" Afina asked.

"I'm sure we could find some men to help us with our bags," Angela said. "And with anything else we needed."

"You two should be on the stage. You're a right pair of comedians."

They drove for a few more minutes, passing the main passenger entrances to the airport. Powell followed the signs for the cargo entrance. He noticed Afina turn and give Angela a quizzical look. Powell pulled to a halt in front of the barrier.

"I don't think we're travelling first class," Angela joked.

After a moment, someone stepped out from the small gate house and opened the rear door of the car. Brian stuck his head inside and said, "Park over there," pointing to a spot in front of a wall.

"What are you doing here?" Angela asked but Brian had already closed the door.

The barrier came up and Powell parked as instructed.

By the time they had all exited the car, Brian was waiting for them.

"This really is a surprise," Angela said, kissing Brian on each cheek.

"Good to see you, Angela," Brian said. He turned to Afina for a hug and further kisses. "Is Powell behaving himself?"

Afina smiled. "Most of the time."

"Are we on time?" Powell asked as he shook hands.

"We have a few minutes."

"So what is this big surprise?" Angela asked. "You really have me intrigued."

"Follow me," Brian instructed. He turned and headed into the building where they had parked.

They all climbed two sets of stairs and Brian led the way to a closed door with a man standing outside. He looked official and gave a curt nod to Brian before holding the door open for them all to enter.

The room was empty and rather drab. Whitewashed walls were turning grey and an old table was the only furniture.

Brian took out his phone and pressed on a contact. "We are in position."

Afina and Angela looked in turn from Brian to Powell. Neither man's face gave nothing away.

"Come to the window," Brian said.

They did as suggested and gazed out on an area where various cargo planes were sitting on the tarmac. After a minute, a small group of people started walking towards one of the planes.

"What are we meant to be looking at?" Angela asked.

Half way across the tarmac the group stopped. A woman emerged from the group and turned back towards the building. Angela gasped as she realised there were two children holding the woman's hands. The woman looked up towards the window and smiled. Then she gave a small wave.

"Is that...?" Afina asked.

Powell smiled and nodded.

After a few seconds two of the men accompanying the woman said something and she turned and continued on her way to the plane. Angela stood transfixed, staring out of the window until everyone boarded the plane.

"You bastards!" Angela swore as she finally turned back from the window. "I've hardly stopped crying for three weeks."

"Sorry," Brian apologised. "We weren't going to let you know the truth but Rose insisted. She wouldn't leave until you knew they were all safe. She said she didn't want to scar you for life.,"

"Where is she going?" Rose asked. Then added quickly, "Sorry, I know you can't tell me."

"So you liked my surprise?" Powell asked.

"Very much," Angela replied. "Will they be all right? If they need money, I can make funds available."

"They will be fine," Powell answered. "They are being relocated under a witness protection program. The government is very grateful to Rose for uncovering her husband's criminal activities and are setting them up in a new life. As a bonus, George unwittingly gave them one hundred thousand pounds in cash. My friend Samurai also diverted a further fifty thousand pounds from one of George's savings accounts. They won't be rich but they will be comfortable."

"And George believes they have all been killed in a car accident?" Angela quizzed.

"Rose and her two children *were* killed in a car accident," Brian emphasised.

"I understand," Angela replied. "But how did you fake their deaths?"

"We had two taxis," Powell explained. "And it was Jenkins doing the shooting. He made Carter keep his head down while we pulled the swap. The car on fire had dummies in the seats. As I jumped out, I pressed a switch and it all went up in flames. Brian and I did something similar many years ago. The only way for Rose to be truly free from her husband was for him to believe she and the children were dead."

Tears were running down Angela's face. "I regretted having introduced you to Rose," she admitted. "Not that for a second I blamed you for what happened. I blamed myself. I'm just so happy how this has turned out."

"Then stop crying," Brian said. "It's worked out well for everyone."

"I'm not sure George Carter would agree with you," Powell laughed.

"Would you like a cigarette?" Afina asked Angela, rummaging in her handbag and taking out a packet.

"I don't smoke," Angela replied.

Afina took a cigarette from the packet and put it between her lips. She delved again into her bag and came out with a lighter. "There are just some times when you have to have a smoke. One won't kill you." Afina lit the cigarette and handed it to Angela.

"I think you're right, Afina. This is one of those moments."

Afina lit a second cigarette and inhaled deeply.

"I thought you gave up," Powell commented.

"And I thought we agreed never to lie to each other. We've only been going out for less than a month and already you are keeping secrets from me. You should have told me, Rose and the children weren't dead."

"That was my fault," Brian interjected. "Powell suggested telling you but I vetoed the idea. It goes against all protocol."

"Brian, I love you but I don't give a damn about protocol. If Powell wants to sleep with me, he has to promise never to lie to me again."

Angela and Brian both turned their heads towards Powell.

"I'm sorry," Powell apologised. "I couldn't tell Angela and I didn't want to put you in the difficult position of having to lie."

"Whatever your reasons. I expect complete honesty."

"Powell, you better hang on to this girl," Angela advised. "She's special."

"I know," Powell agreed.

"Now I have that off my chest," Afina said. "We should head back to the bar. We have had our first argument and I need to remind Powell what he will be missing, if he ever lies to me again."

EPILOGUE

Powell was at home watching the evening news on television when he heard about the death of George Carter. The former MP, who had resigned in tragic circumstances, was found dead at home. Powell listened intently to the news item. Carter appeared to have committed suicide by taking an overdose of pills.

Powell picked up his phone and called Brian. "I've just seen Carter has committed suicide. Is that for real?"

"There is no evidence to suggest otherwise. It would be perfectly understandable and frankly, no one is going to shed any tears."

Powell remembered his conversation with Brian, where he revealed it was possible once they had extracted all useful information from Carter, he would meet an untimely end. Equally, it could be the Chairman who was responsible. Powell decided he preferred not to know the truth. The man was dead either way.

"What about the Chairman? Did you find out who he is?" Powell asked.

"Yes. I won't name him on an open line but it turns out he's American. Given he is one of the richest and most influential men in the world, we directly briefed the President. We weren't sure who else we could trust."

"Has the President taken action?"

"Seems he's reluctant. There is no evidence of any crime."

"Why am I not surprised?"

"Anyway, the President has more pressing problems. The Russians are stirring up unrest in the Baltic. Putin's set light to the touch paper and there is going to be fireworks."

"Closer to home, what happens to all Carter's money now he is dead?"

"Not sure."

"It would be good if Rose and the children could receive a fair chunk."

"That might be difficult. Seeing how they are all officially dead."

"They deserve the money. Can't you find a way to divert some funds? I'm sure Samurai could help if necessary."

"I'll look into it but I'm making no promises."

"Did you manage to let Rose know he was dead before she could see it on the news?"

"I'm afraid we didn't," Brian said apologetically. "The news broke too quickly. By the time I was informed, it was too late. I don't suppose she will lose any sleep over his death."

"No. I only hope the children didn't learn about their father's death on the news. I'll give Angela a call in case she hasn't seen the news."

"You should come up to town for a lunch," Brian encouraged. "I'm buying. I have another matter I want to pass by you."

"If you're buying lunch it must be bloody dangerous! Want to give me a clue?"

"Not over the phone. "

"Is it urgent? Only I was thinking of taking a long holiday with Afina."

"It can wait a couple of weeks but not much longer."

THE END

Also by Bill Ward

Powell series:

Trafficking

Abducted

Deception

Betrayed

Retribution

Stand-alone thrillers:

Revenge

Encryption

TRAFFICKING
Powell Book 1

Trafficking is big business and those involved show no remorse, have no mercy, only a deadly intent to protect their income.

Afina is a young Romanian girl with high expectations when she arrives in Brighton but she has been tricked and there is no job, only a life as a sex slave.

Facing a desperate future, Afina tries to escape and a young female police officer, who comes to her aid, is stabbed.

Powell's life has been torn apart for the second time and he is determined to find the man responsible for his daughter's death.

Action, violence and sex abound in this taut thriller about one of today's worst crimes.

5* Reviews

"This book is not for the faint hearted but it is a brilliant read."

"Keeps you at the edge of your seat throughout."

"Exciting, terrifying, brilliant."

"One of the best books I have read in a long time!"

"Will leave you breathless."

ABDUCTED
Powell Book 2

Powell returns in an action packed novel of violence, sex and betrayal!

He is trying to recover two children from Saudi Arabia, who have been abducted by their father.

In a culture where women are second class citizens, a woman holds the key to the success or failure of his mission.

Meanwhile, back in Brighton, Afina is trying to deal with a new threat from Romanian gangsters.

From the streets of Brighton to Riyadh, Powell must take the law into his own hands, to help the innocent.

5* Reviews

"Trafficking was masterful and this one is even better."

"Great thriller."

"Fabulous twists and turns."

"Strong, interesting characters."

DECEPTION
Powell Book 3

The Americans aren't happy with the changing political climate in Britain. Elements of the CIA and MI6 enter into a conspiracy to help shape the thinking of the British public.

Meanwhile ISIS has a plan to bring terror to the streets of Britain.

Powell is caught in the middle when he offers help to a former lover, whose life is in danger. Soon it becomes evident, someone will stop at nothing to see them both silenced.

Unsure who can be trusted, Powell must act to save the lives of his friends and right a terrible wrong.

5* Reviews

"Couldn't put the book down it was so gripping."

"Brilliant, like his other books, can't wait for his next book.."

"A thrill on every page."

"A real thriller, action, suspense, and a well thought out plot. All in all a good, gripping read. More Powell books please."

BETRAYED
Powell Book 4

Powell returns in an action packed story of a commune, drugs and corrupt police officers.

Scott, the charismatic leader of the commune, promotes free love and the sharing of wealth.

Hattie is a twenty year old about to inherit a £25m fortune and her parents are worried about the influence Scott exerts on their impressionable daughter. Family ties will be tested to the limits.

Powell is hired to infiltrate the commune but finds himself framed for murder and on the run. Tired of being on the back foot he decides it is time to go on the offensive.

Betrayal is rife and sometimes from the most unexpected quarters.

5* Reviews

"Powell is becoming one of my favourite characters. Always a gripping read with lots of suspense."

"Fans of suspense, edge of your seat, fast-paced action thrillers should read this book and the other four."

"Another superb read from Bill Ward."

"I have really enjoyed the Powell series books. I haven't been able to put them down."

RETRIBUTION
Powell Book 5

Powell has a temporary job as a bodyguard protecting Bob Hale, the local Member of Parliament, who is a senior member of the team negotiating Britain's exit from the EU.

Someone wants Hale dead. Powell suspects the motive may not be political. Is there a dark secret in Hale's past? Powerful men will stop at nothing to prevent Powell discovering the truth.

In an emotional story of abuse and lost innocence, Powell must again walk a tightrope between the law and delivering justice.

5* Reviews

" I do hope it's not the last we'll see of Powell."

"Omg amazing book once again Bill Ward has kept me up all night."

"I'm a fan of this author."

"Another gripping instalment in the Powell series."

"A cracking read full of really interesting and real characters!"

REVENGE.

There is no greater motivator for evil than a huge sense of injustice!

Tom Ashdown, an unlikely hero, owns a betting shop in Brighton and gambles with his life when he stumbles across an attempted kidnapping, which leaves him entangled in a dangerous chain of events involving the IRA, a sister seeking revenge for the death of her brother and an informer in MI5 with a secret in his past.

Revenge is a fast paced thriller, with twists and turns at every step.

In a thrilling and violent climax everyone is intent on some form of revenge.

5* Reviews

"Fast paced from the start and it only goes faster!"

"This novel is a real page turner!"

"It will keep you on the edge of your seat."

"Revenge is an example of everything that I look for in an action thriller."

ENCRYPTION.

In a small software engineering company in England, a game changing algorithm for encrypting data has been invented, which will have far reaching consequences for the fight against terrorism.

The Security Services of the UK, USA and China all want to control the new software.

The Financial Director has been murdered and his widow turns to her brother-in-law to help discover the truth. But he soon finds himself framed for his brother's murder.

When the full force of government is brought to bear on one family, they seem to face impossible odds. Is it an abuse of power or does the end justify the means?

Only one man can find the answers but he is being hunted by the same people he once called friends and colleagues.

5* Reviews

"A Great English Spy Thriller."

"This is a great story! Once I started reading it, I could not put it down."

"Full of memorable characters and enough twists and turns to impress all diehard thriller junkies, it is a wonderful read"

"If you're a fan of Ludlum, and love descriptive prose like that of Michener, you'll be right at home."

ABOUT THE AUTHOR

Bill Ward has recently moved from Brighton and now lives in Nottingham with his German partner Anja. He has retired from senior corporate roles in large IT companies and is following a lifelong passion for writing! With 7 daughters, a son, stepson, 2 horses, a dog and 2 cats, life is always busy!

Bill's other great passion is supporting West Bromwich Albion, which he has been doing for more than 50 years!

Connect with Bill online:

Twitter: http://twitter.com/billward10bill

Facebook: http://facebook.com/billwardbooks

Printed in Great Britain
by Amazon